"Your train derailed. You were airlifted here to the hospital."

So far, Wade had given her only fragments of her life, certainly not enough for her to piece together her identity, but too much for a total stranger to know. She studied his face with more care than before, seeing past the composed veneer to a restless energy beneath. "Do I know you?"

"We've never met."

Confusion made her head ache. "Then why are you here with me?"

"Maybe the rest can wait." He avoided her eyes.

"Tell me now. Why are you being so attentive to someone you've never met?"

He raised his head and caught her in the powerful gaze of eyes so deep and murky she could have drowned in them.

"Because you were going to marry me."

Dear Reader,

Welcome to Harlequin American Romance...where each month we offer four wonderful new books bursting with love!

Linda Randall Wisdom kicks off the month with *Bride of Dreams*, the latest installment in the RETURN TO TYLER series, in which a handsome Native American lawman is undeniably drawn to the pretty and mysterious new waitress in town. Watch for the Tyler series to continue next month in Harlequin Historicals. Next, a lovely schoolteacher is in for a big surprise when she wakes up in a hospital with no memory of her past—or how she'd gotten pregnant. Meet the last of the three identical sisters in Muriel Jensen's WHO'S THE DADDY? series in *Father Found*.

Bestselling author Judy Christenberry's *Rent a Millionaire Groom* launches Harlequin American Romance's new series, 2001 WAYS TO WED, about three best friends searching for Mr. Right who turn to a book guaranteed to help them make it to the altar. IDENTITY SWAP, Charlotte Douglas's new cross-line series, debuts with *Montana Mail-Order Wife*. In this exciting story, two women involved in a train accident switch identities and find much more than they bargained for. Follow the series next month in Harlequin Intrigue.

Enjoy this month's offerings, and make sure to return each and every month to Harlequin American Romance!

Wishing you happy reading,

Melissa Jeglinski
Associate Senior Editor
Harlequin American Romance

MONTANA
MAIL-ORDER WIFE
Charlotte Douglas

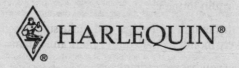

HARLEQUIN®

TORONTO • NEW YORK • LONDON
AMSTERDAM • PARIS • SYDNEY • HAMBURG
STOCKHOLM • ATHENS • TOKYO • MILAN • MADRID
PRAGUE • WARSAW • BUDAPEST • AUCKLAND

For the brave men and women who fought
the Montana wildfires of the summer of 2000.

ISBN 0-373-16868-3

MONTANA MAIL-ORDER WIFE

ABOUT THE AUTHOR

Charlotte Douglas has loved a good story since she learned to read at the age of three. After years of teaching that love of books to her students, she now enjoys creating stories of her own. Often her books are set in one of her three favorite places: Montana, where she and her husband spent their honeymoon, the mountains of North Carolina where they're building a summer home, and Florida, near the Gulf of Mexico on Florida's west coast, where she's lived most of her life.

Books by Charlotte Douglas

HARLEQUIN AMERICAN ROMANCE
591—IT'S ABOUT TIME
623—BRINGING UP BABY
868—MONTANA MAIL-ORDER WIFE*

HARLEQUIN INTRIGUE
380—DREAM MAKER
434—BEN'S WIFE
482—FIRST-CLASS FATHER
515—A WOMAN OF MYSTERY
536—UNDERCOVER DAD

* Identity Swap

Don't miss any of our special offers. Write to us at the following address for information on our newest releases.

Harlequin Reader Service
U.S.: 3010 Walden Ave., P.O. Box 1325, Buffalo, NY 14269
Canadian: P.O. Box 609, Fort Erie, Ont. L2A 5X3

NEWS FLASH SPECIAL REPORT!

We interrupt your regularly scheduled program to bring you this breaking news.

A Westward Railways train has derailed just outside Kalispell. Police have reported several injuries, mostly minor. Several passengers have been taken to local area hospitals.

One young woman, traveling alone, identified as Rachel O'Riley, is suffering from a concussion and what appears to be amnesia. Her fiancé has been contacted by local authorities and is at her bedside.

Only one passenger is unaccounted for—another young woman identified from her ticket receipt as Jennifer Reid. Police have called off the search, as they believe she was unharmed in the accident and left the scene. Her whereabouts and her destination are unknown....

Chapter One

Wade Garrett awoke with a start, jerked upright in his chair and slammed his boots from the windowsill to the floor. Perspiration speckled his forehead, and his heart raced from the still-vivid nightmare. His son had been lost and calling to him, but he couldn't find the boy anywhere.

He rubbed his eyes and shoved his fingers through his hair. Only a dream. Jordan was fine, at home with Ursula.

Rolling his shoulders to stretch his stiff muscles, he hoisted himself from the depths of the chair he'd slept in for the past two nights. A quick glance assured him he hadn't disturbed the still figure in the hospital bed beside him. Rachel O'Riley lay bruised, battered and comatose, and in her vulnerable state, she tugged at his heartstrings, reminding him of his son, an angel when asleep.

Jordan, an angel?

Wade grimaced with bitter humor. Jordan awake was a holy terror. And Jordan was the reason Wade kept vigil in Rachel O'Riley's hospital room.

He stumbled through the predawn twilight into

the tiny bathroom. At the lavatory he sluiced cold water over his face to drive away the dregs of sleep, raised his head and confronted a memory in the mirror.

Six years ago he'd spent several nights in a hospital room, not caring then, either, about unkempt hair, eyes red rimmed with fatigue, or the three-day stubble on his chin. Maggie had been dying from complications of a stillbirth, and he'd kept watch, consumed with anger and pain at the circumstances that had brought her there.

Déjà vu.

Except the woman in the hospital bed wasn't Maggie. She wasn't dying. And he wasn't angry. Or in pain. Why should he be? He'd never laid eyes on Rachel O'Riley until Sheriff Howard called him to the hospital after finding Wade's name and address in her backpack.

Wade scowled at his mirror image, scrubbed his face dry with a rough paper towel and turned away, unwilling to admit, even to himself, that the mysterious Rachel had triggered a deep reaction and stirred emotions he had believed, *hoped,* had atrophied and died with Maggie. With the demands of the ranch and raising eight-year-old Jordan, he had no time for sentimental entanglements.

He swished cold water in his mouth, spit as if to expel his unwanted thoughts, and longed for hot, black coffee. A solid jolt of caffeine should banish his outlandish notions.

When he came out of the bathroom, the day nurse stood beside the bed, taking her patient's pulse and making notes on a chart. Her round, pleasant face broke into a smile. "Good morning, Mr. Garrett."

Wade nodded toward the bed. "How is she?"

"Her vital signs are strong. The doctor's certain she'll regain consciousness soon."

When he headed toward his chair, the nurse waved him away. "You're the one we're worried about. Not enough sleep or food to keep a bird alive, much less a big man like you. Get some breakfast in the cafeteria. I'll page you if there's any change."

Wade scrutinized Rachel, quiescent and pale, so slight her body barely mounded the hospital blanket above the mattress. Her tranquil face fired his interest in a disturbing way. High, sculpted cheekbones as ashen as her pillow were framed by thick blond hair that reminded him of his prize palomino in the sunlight. She had the kind of hair a man liked to run his fingers through.

The surprising sweetness of her bow-shaped mouth and the gracefulness of feathery brows arching across her smooth, high forehead were details her letters had omitted.

Her chatty correspondence had left him unmoved, so he'd been unprepared for the tightening in his gut and the heat surging through his blood at seeing her for the first time.

And every time he'd looked at her since.

Gritting his teeth until his jaw ached, he ignored the unwelcome hankering and squelched his preoccupation with her stunning face.

He'd need a whole bucket of coffee to purge the sentiment cluttering his mind—and the hormones tormenting his body.

He was overreacting to the woman because he was bone-tired, he assured himself. What he felt was only sympathy, same as he'd feel for anybody banged up as she'd been in the train accident. Once she was on her feet again and he'd had a good night's rest, his emotional balance would return. Then he could handle the demands of the ranch he'd let slide since Sheriff Howard had called to say he was needed at the county hospital.

"You okay, Mr. Garrett?" the nurse asked.

She'd caught him gawking at Rachel like he was plumb weak north of his ears. He'd been under too much stress lately, what with Jordan's troubles and the extra workload at the ranch, and his moonstruck behavior proved it.

"Call me if there's any change." Striding from the room, he ignored the impulse for one last glance.

He halted at the pay phone in the hall and dialed home. Ursula's gravelly voice greeted him. "How is she?"

"Doc says she should be okay, but she hasn't regained consciousness yet." He massaged a crick in his neck. "Is Jordan staying out of trouble?"

The old housekeeper's initial hesitation told him more than her words. "He's fine. Just keeps asking when his daddy's coming home."

A mixture of guilt and frustration scoured through him, and he cursed silently. After all, the boy was the reason he was here. "I'll be home tonight."

"Are you going to tell him?"

He pretended not to understand. "About the train wreck?"

Ursula's ironic expletive burst in his ear. "You know what I mean."

"I'll tell him. Eventually."

He hung up the receiver and rammed his hands in his pockets. Trouble always came in threes. First Jordan's rebellion, then the train derailment. God only knew what was next. The disturbing speculation accompanied him all the way to the cafeteria.

SHE NOTICED THE SOUNDS first. The clanking of an ice machine across the hall, the whir of rubberized wheels on a linoleum floor, hushed voices outside the door. And a strange, unrelenting pounding.

She lay quiet, eyes closed, absorbing the unfamiliar noises. The other sounds diminished, but the pounding persisted as blood rushed through her veins and her temples throbbed. She struggled against a consuming weakness and opened her eyes.

Directly above, a metal track etched the white ceiling. Her gaze followed it to the wall, where a muslin curtain was gathered back beside the bed. Beside her, a plastic bag hung from an aluminum stand, and clear tubing filled with fluid snaked from it to her wrist. When she flexed her left hand, a needle pinched her vein.

She was in a hospital.

She gazed through a wide window across from the bed at a broad, boulder-filled river, frothy with whitewater tinted pink by the sun's slanting rays. Beyond the river, a stand of towering evergreens formed an impenetrable barricade. She knotted her forehead in concentration, but try as she might, she couldn't identify where she was or whether the sun was rising or setting.

Her next discovery banished all thoughts of time or place. A thirty-something man sprawled in the chair beside the window, sound asleep. Who was he?

Her doctor?

He was dressed more like a cowboy, in well-worn jeans that enveloped long legs, a chambray shirt stretched taut over powerful muscles, and tooled leather boots that could stand a good polish. The sun streaks in his mahogany-colored hair and the tanned, rugged planes of his attractive face suggested someone who worked outdoors.

She flushed when she realized he'd awakened during her scrutiny and was staring back with eyes as serene and brown as the river boulders outside the window.

"Welcome back." His agreeable voice rolled through the room, a rich baritone.

"Back?" She attempted to draw herself to a sitting position, but the effort exhausted her and she collapsed against the pillows.

"You've been unconscious almost three days." He shoved himself to his feet in a graceful movement and approached her bed with the rolling gait of a man more comfortable on a horse than on his feet.

Giddiness and disorientation washed over her. "What happened?"

He hooked his thumbs in the back pockets of his jeans and lifted dark eyebrows with a look so galvanizing she averted her eyes. "You don't remember?"

"No." She fidgeted beneath his piercing inspection and wished she was wearing something more substantial than a thin hospital gown.

"I'd better get the doctor." His probing expression relaxed as if he was pleased by an excuse to bolt.

Loneliness and an unnamed yearning overwhelmed her. Between the pounding in her head and the weakness of her body, she couldn't pinpoint who—or what—she longed for. All she knew was that she didn't want to be alone.

"Please, don't go," she begged.

The skin around his eyes crinkled in appealing lines and his mouth angled in a reassuring smile. He reached above her pillow and depressed a call button.

"Nurses' station," a chirpy voice responded.

"Tell Dr. Sinclair Miss O'Riley is awake," he said.

"That's good news," the voice said. "I'll page the doctor."

When he started to move away, she grasped his sleeve. "Who's Miss O'Riley?"

He frowned before composing his face into a neutral expression. "Don't you know?"

Her misgivings multiplied by the second. She concentrated on the tenacious squareness of his jaw, the dark hair tumbling across his broad forehead, a tiny scar across one dark eyebrow—anything to block the other questions that assaulted her.

The one about O'Riley terrified her enough.

She gathered her courage with a deep breath. "Who is Miss O'Riley?"

His widened eyes conveyed his surprise. "You are."

The answer stunned her, and the questions she'd tried to evade converged until she slipped again toward the black void from which she'd just emerged. In a futile attempt to conquer confusion, she thrashed her aching head from side to side on the pillow.

"Whoa, hold still." The stranger cupped her cheeks with firm but gentle hands. "You've had a bad concussion. You don't want to aggravate it."

Closing her eyes to avoid his warm, searching gaze, she relaxed against the soothing pressure of his palms. "You don't understand."

"Try me."

His simple, direct proposal inspired her trust. When she opened her eyes, tears misted her vision, and she observed the stranger through a watery haze.

"I don't *know* who I am." She choked back panic. "I can't remember anything."

"Nothing?" he asked, as if disbelieving.

Her throat tightened with anxiety, and she clasped his hands as if they were a lifeline. "Not even my own name."

He freed himself from her grasp, fumbled in his shirt pocket and pulled out a letter. "Maybe this will jog your memory. It's from you."

She seized the pages and scanned the lines of looping scrawl, but nothing connected. No name, no remembrances. She blinked back tears of frustration. "This means nothing to me."

More concerned with the stranger than the letter, she handed back the pages. Reeling from lack of memory, she battled her befuddling attraction to the good-looking man.

A disturbing possibility struck her. "Who are you?"

"Wade Garrett."

She glanced at her left hand and her unadorned ring finger. "That's a relief. I thought for a moment you might be *Mr.* O'Riley."

"No."

The mysterious glint in his eye intrigued her, but his lack of information was irritating. "Are you related to me?"

He shook his head.

Her disappointment stung. Wade appeared to be the kind of man she could lean on in a crisis—not only physically strong, with broad shoulders and hard muscles, but with a disposition that didn't rattle easily.

If he wasn't her relative or her husband…a tremor shook her at the very idea…who was he? "Do I know you?"

"Not yet."

Behind a facade of calm, she hid her irritation at his refusal to provide more information. Obviously he wasn't ready to tell her why he was here, but maybe he'd answer other questions.

Again she experienced the unsettling but source-less longing. "What about my family?"

Uncertainty flickered over his handsome face. "We'll discuss your family later."

Between the ache in her temples and an avalanche

of unanswered questions, she couldn't think straight. The mysterious Wade Garrett, talking in generalities, was no help at all.

Fatigue depleted her last reserves of strength, and she closed her eyes. Maybe she was only dreaming, and once she awoke, she'd remember everything she was supposed to, including who she was and what part Wade Garrett played in her life.

All she wanted now was sleep.

WADE WATCHED HER DRIFT into unconsciousness again. He'd been totally unprepared for the impact of those eyes, the deep pine-green of a ponderosa, and so wide they almost swallowed her face. And her kick-in-the-gut smile had almost done him in, especially when he noted the fleeting unhappiness beneath it. That look reminded him of a stray dog Jordan had adopted years ago after its human family moved away and left it behind.

Maybe, like Shep, the woman would need lots of care before her loneliness left her. Wade's thoughts snarled like barbed wire as he combed his fingers through his hair and massaged his neck, stiff again from sleeping in the chair. She hadn't mentioned any unhappiness in her letters. And love definitely wasn't part of their deal.

But she looked so vulnerable, lying there asleep, that he couldn't resist reaching for her hand, fingers curled like a half-opened blossom atop the blanket. At the contact with her warm, smooth skin, testosterone bucked through his blood like an untamed mustang.

When the doctor entered, Wade jerked his hand

away and blushed like a green adolescent caught necking on the porch.

Dr. Sinclair, a tiny, birdlike woman with enough nervous energy to power a city, marched to the bed and checked Rachel's pulse. She removed a penlight from the pocket of her white coat, lifted Rachel's eyelids and examined her pupils.

Straightening as if her back ached, the doctor brushed a strand of salt-and-pepper hair from her forehead and confronted Wade. "Did she speak to you?"

"Briefly." Long enough for him to learn her voice was as soft as a mountain breeze.

"Was she lucid?"

"She was rational, if that's what you mean."

The doctor's shrewd gaze skewered him. "What aren't you telling me, Mr. Garrett?"

"Her memory's gone."

Her intense blue eyes behind gold-framed glasses gave nothing away, and she gestured toward the door.

He followed her into the hall before posing his question. "Is it a brain injury?"

Dr. Sinclair shook her head and stuffed her stethoscope into her pocket. "CAT scan and EEG are both normal, now that her concussion is subsiding."

He rammed his fingers through his hair. He hadn't expected this crimp in his plans. He should have been halfway home by now, as he'd promised Jordan, but how could he leave Rachel alone and frightened, not knowing who she was? "Why can't she remember?"

"She suffered a bad bump on the back of her

head. Amnesia caused by physical trauma should clear up within a couple of days.''

He expelled a sigh of relief. ''So she'll be all right?''

''Unless we're dealing with hysteria.''

He frowned. ''She seemed calm enough. But she did shed a few tears.''

Dr. Sinclair smiled and shook her head. ''Not that kind of hysteria. Amnesia caused by psychological trauma. Imagine what she experienced, plunging into that deep ravine in a tumbling, burning railroad car.''

Wade nodded. Rachel had been air-lifted to Libby, partly because Wade was there, but mostly because the Kalispell hospital was filled to capacity with other wreck victims. He jerked his wandering attention back to the doctor.

''Her mind may be protecting her from reexperiencing that nightmare by shutting down her memories.''

''But she'll get them back?''

Sinclair patted his hand, reminding him of his long-dead mother. ''In a few days, *if* her memory loss is due to physical trauma.''

''And if it isn't?''

''When she's strong enough to face the memories.''

''Soon?''

The little doctor shrugged. ''Maybe the next time she awakens, maybe in a few days.'' Her voice had an upward inflection, hinting of things left unsaid.

''Or?''

Dr. Sinclair avoided his eyes. ''Maybe never.''

"Never? But you said there's no permanent injury to her brain—"

"In spite of medical advances, many mysteries of the human mind are still unsolved." Her smile didn't hide her weariness. "But you're worrying prematurely. She may recall everything when she awakes again."

"And if she doesn't?"

"Her memories could come rushing back anytime, or they could return gradually in bits and pieces."

He glanced into the room at the sleeping Rachel. If she didn't remember soon, she'd be in for a rough time. She'd need care, attention and reassurance. The prospect of providing for her warmed him— until his common sense kicked in.

Feelings played no part in their relationship, and Jordan was enough to worry about. Rachel was supposed to ease his troubles, not add to them.

He hardened his heart and looked away. No point in worrying about what only time could cure. He glanced at his watch. If he hurried, he might reach home before Jordan's bedtime. "What about her family?"

Dr. Sinclair shook her head. "The local authorities traced her to Atlanta, then back to Missouri. Her parents are deceased. She was their only child."

"No aunts or uncles, cousins?"

The doctor shook her head. "Not that they could find."

"What about close friends?"

"There's no one."

The tenderness he'd tried to suppress surged through him. "Poor kid."

"I wouldn't say that." Dr. Sinclair patted his hand again. "After all, she has you."

Chapter Two

"Rachel."

Sitting up in bed, she shaped the alien name with her lips, but it lacked familiarity.

She grimaced in disgust. So what else was new? *Nothing* seemed familiar. Nothing except her face in the mirror. She choked back a derisive laugh. What a big help. She recognized herself.

When she'd awakened this morning, she'd thought at first she'd dreamed Wade Garrett and her amnesia, until she had to admit her encounter with Wade was the *only* memory she possessed.

He'd said they weren't related and had never met. But who was he?

Some religious zealot dedicating his life to visiting the sick? She quickly rejected that idea. The man had too much devil in his deep brown eyes.

Maybe he was a plainclothes policeman. Had she been fleeing some crime when her train crashed? After her heart stopped thundering in her chest, she discarded that possibility, too. Although she couldn't remember, she could still *feel,* and she didn't feel like a criminal.

In frustration, she pounded her pillow with her fists. No use wondering who Wade Garrett was when she'd probably never see him again.

The thought gave her no comfort.

"Rachel. Rachel O'Riley."

She repeated the name, hoping to trigger a response, but her mind remained a wasteland, barren of any recollection except the most mundane.

"The doctor says fresh air will do you good." Wade Garrett lounged in the doorway of her room, one elbow propped against the doorjamb, the thumb of his other hand tucked in the low-slung waistband of his jeans.

His sudden appearance delighted and annoyed her, immobilizing her with indecision. "Who are you?"

His intriguing face crumpled with dismay. "Don't you remember?"

"I know you're Wade Garrett," she said with impatience, "but what do you have to do with *me?*"

"You feel up to a walk around the grounds?" His slow smile heated up the room.

"If I walk with you, will you answer my question?"

He regarded her solemnly for a moment, then nodded.

A younger, more handsome version of the Marlboro Man, that's who he reminded her of, with his chiseled features, sun-streaked hair and wind-burned skin. Another useless bit of information remembered. She clenched her fists in frustration at the quickening of her pulse and the flush that seared her cheeks.

Hoping to fill the emptiness with his presence, she couldn't deny she'd been waiting for him all morning. But only for what he could tell her, she assured herself. Her racing blood and somersaulting stomach at the sight of the stranger were due strictly to her thirst for information. Neither Dr. Sinclair nor the nurses would tell her anything, but maybe Wade could furnish the facts she couldn't recall.

She forced a smile with more bravery than she felt. After all, he'd promised answers. "I'd take you up on that walk, but my legs are a bit shaky."

They'd gotten a whole lot shakier since he arrived.

His gaze scanned her legs, from the bottom of her short hospital gown to her ankles, crossed atop the covers. "They look fine to me."

Her misgivings melted as the heat in his dark eyes transferred to the pit of her stomach. In a futile effort, she tugged at the hem of her gown. No sense going all warm and snuggly over Wade Garrett, when, for all she knew, she had a husband and three kids somewhere, waiting for her to come home.

Home.

Where *was* home? And what was she doing here, fighting the desire to throw herself into a tall stranger's arms and have him take care of her?

She swung her legs off the bed on the side away from Wade and tugged on the shapeless cotton robe the hospital had provided. Shaky legs or not, she'd accompany him until he'd given her some explanations. She slid her feet into frumpy hospital slippers and stood on wobbly limbs.

In an instant, Wade was beside her, gripping her elbow to steady her. "Lean on me."

She jumped at his touch and would have fallen if he hadn't grabbed her.

What was the matter with her? Why had she hopped like water on a hot griddle at the pressure of his hand? She glanced into bottomless brown eyes that registered his confusion at her reaction. He'd offered a simple gesture of help and thoughtful words. She'd responded as if he'd electrocuted her.

Bewilderment brought tears to her eyes. She dashed them away with the back of her hand. Undeterred, Wade reached for her elbow again, but she shook off his assistance, hesitant to be indebted to a man she knew nothing about.

"I'll be okay." She didn't sound convincing, even to herself.

Ignoring her protest, he slid an arm around her waist and bore the brunt of her weight. She would have protested further, but without his support, her legs would have buckled.

With Wade's help, she shuffled into the hallway. He nodded toward the exit at the end of the hall. "The hospital garden's just past those doors."

She traversed the hall, aware of the searing heat of Wade's strong hip pressed against her torso. She forced weak muscles to carry her forward, and Wade matched his pace to hers. When she stepped from beneath the entrance portico, morning sunlight toasted her face, banishing the chill of air conditioning.

If only it could unlock her memories as well.

She glanced up at the stranger at her side, hoping he held the key to who she was. If he did, he exhibited no haste to reveal it. A shiver joined the trembling in her legs. Maybe he was hiding something, something she wouldn't want to hear.

She chastised herself for her fears. Surely nothing could be worse than not knowing. She'd make him tell. The sooner the better.

Bolstered by Wade's strong arm, she ambled along the brick path through elliptical pools of shade cast by tall Douglas firs. Intent on the enigmatic man at her side, she spared only a cursory glance for the deep purple petunias and mounds of white alyssum that bordered the walk.

When they reached a concrete bench set back from the path under a small maple, he steadied her as she sat, then stepped away.

She drew the cotton robe around her and confronted him. "Isn't it time you answered my questions?"

Seemingly unperturbed by her abruptness, he dropped to the ground with a natural gracefulness, leaned back against the bench and stared across the garden. She couldn't see his eyes, only the angle of his cheek and the silky texture of sun-bleached hair that brushed the top of his collar. A twitching muscle in his jaw betrayed his calm.

"What do you want to know?" Something in his even tone hinted at emotions held firmly in check.

She looked around in confusion at the pine-covered hills rising beyond the river toward a range

of snow-capped mountains in the distance. "Where
am I?"

"You're just outside Libby."

"Where's that?"

"Northwest Montana."

"Do I live here?"

"You were traveling to your new home at Longhorn Lake, less than an hour west of here."

Montana didn't seem familiar, but then nothing
else did, either. Her most pressing question concerned her identity. She leaned forward until she
could watch his expression. "Who *am* I?"

His eyes glowed briefly with a curious longing
before he looked away. "You're Rachel O'Riley."

"That's only a name. Who am I?"

He shifted toward her, grasped her fists clenched
on her lap and smoothed her fingers open with a
gentleness unexpected in such a big man. "You're
coiled tighter than a spring. Dr. Sinclair says you
mustn't get worked up over this."

"How can I *not*—"

"Shh." He lifted his index finger to her lips, creating an unaccustomed tingle along the sensitive
skin. "If you promise to relax, I promise to answer
any questions I can."

His composure irritated her, but his unyielding expression convinced her to follow his instructions.
She inhaled, drawing in the resinous scent of evergreens and the fragrance of unfamiliar flowers on
the cool mountain air. Slowly, her tension eased.

"That's better." He released her hands with a nod
of satisfaction, but his eyes held a burning, distant
look, as if he wished he was anywhere but there.

She resisted the urge to grab his hand again, yearning for his touch to drive away her lack of connection to anyone or anything. "Please, tell me about myself, my family, what I'm doing here."

"You're twenty-eight years old. You grew up in Missouri." With a calm she envied, he ticked off the facts on long, capable fingers with clean, square nails. "You're an only child. Both your parents died years ago in an automobile accident."

His words generated no response.

No memories.

No pain.

He scanned her face as if looking for signs of the recognition she longed for, but she couldn't reveal what wasn't there. For all the impact his words had, he could have been talking about a total stranger.

"And after my parents died?" she prodded.

"A few years ago you sold your home in Missouri and moved to Atlanta."

The breeze changed direction, gusting across Wade, carrying a pleasantly masculine scent of leather and soap and lifting his hair to expose a high, wide forehead, slightly less tanned than his cheeks.

Had she lost her mind as well as her memories? She should be concentrating on the missing facts of her life, not the all-too-fascinating man before her.

"Did I have a job in Atlanta?" She silently cursed the breathlessness in her voice.

Wade didn't seem to notice, but if he did, she hoped he blamed it on curiosity. "You worked as a paralegal in a firm that practiced corporate law."

Corporate law? When she drew another blank at the term, her frustration grew, and she had to force herself to relax again. "What about the rest of my family?"

He shook his head and compassion glittered in his eyes. "There's nobody. The hospital's had the authorities searching for next of kin ever since you were brought here. After the accident."

As if uneasy, he shifted and assessed her with a wary eye, but again she experienced nothing except curiosity in reaction to his words. "What accident?"

"Your train derailed west of Kalispell. You were airlifted to the hospital here."

So far, he'd given her only fragments of her life, certainly not enough for her to piece together her identity, but too much for a total stranger to know. "How do you know so much about me?"

He shrugged, and the compassion in his face gave way to discomfort. "I learned most of it from your letters."

"Letters? Like the one you showed me yesterday?"

He nodded, then sat unmoving, almost as if holding his breath.

She studied his face with more care than before, seeing past the composed veneer to a restless energy beneath. "Do I know you?"

"We've never met."

Confusion made her head ache. "Then why was I writing to you?"

"Maybe the rest can wait." He avoided her eyes.

His evasiveness alarmed her and made her pulse quicken. The rest had been dry facts, meaningless, but she could tell from the tension in his posture that this answer was crucial. "Tell me now. Why was I writing to someone I've never met?"

He raised his head and caught her in the powerful gaze of eyes so deep and murky she could have drowned in them.

"Because you were going to marry me."

WADE SCRAMBLED to his feet and caught the fainting Rachel before she slid off the bench. As he jogged back toward the building with her in his arms, her thick lashes brushed cheeks gone pale, and her warm, supple body bounced, featherlight, against his chest. A fierce protectiveness flared deep in his gut, white-hot with forgotten longing.

You scared her to death, you dadburned fool. Maybe her promise to marry you is something she doesn't want to remember.

The automatic door glided open at his approach. He rushed past the nurses' station to her room and laid her on the bed. Drawing the covers to hide her long, sculpted legs, slender hips and the firm, round curves of her breasts from his covetous glance, he stepped back and shoved hands that ached to touch her into his pockets.

He was acting like such a damned idiot, no wonder she'd fainted at the thought of marrying him. Between the train wreck and her amnesia, she'd already suffered too many shocks. News of their engagement had been the last straw. Guilt seeped through him for telling her so abruptly.

And tenderness followed as he noted the sweet curve of her cheek against the pillow, reminding him of countless times he'd carried a sleeping Jordan to his room and tucked him in without waking him.

Ah, Jordan. I thought I'd worked out everything for you, and now look what I've gone and done.

"Will she be okay?" He shifted aside for the nurse to check Rachel.

Rachel's lids fluttered, and she opened her eyes. "I'm fine. Just a little tired."

The nurse concurred with Rachel's assessment. "But no more outings until tomorrow. In the meantime, rest."

Rachel propped herself on her elbows, watched the door close behind the nurse, then turned amazing emerald eyes toward him. "Sorry if I worried you. I'm fine, really."

Weak with relief, he grinned. "Coulda fooled me. I thought you'd gone into cardiac arrest at the mention of marriage."

A delightful blush brought the pinkness back to her cheeks, and a dancing smile brightened her eyes. "You're the first man who's ever proposed to me." Her smile dimmed. "That I can remember, anyway."

His face flamed with discomfort. Because she couldn't recall the circumstances of their engagement, she'd jumped to all the wrong conclusions.

Not that he blamed her.

Ever since she'd first met him, she couldn't help noticing the unintended signals of his unexpected and definitely unwelcome attraction to her that he'd been relaying like a microwave tower. He had to set her straight before she embarrassed herself, or him, further.

He dragged a straight chair beside the bed, straddled it backward, and folded his arms on the backrest. Explaining in a letter would have been a lot easier, without his tongue wrapping itself around his teeth. And without the distraction of too-green eyes, kissable lips and a pert nose turned up at just the right angle.

"My, uh, proposal," he said, "isn't what you think."

She had punched the automatic control and raised the head of the bed so her face was even with his. At his disclaimer, she grew so still that, if her eyes hadn't blinked, he would have sworn she'd gone comatose again.

"If your proposal isn't what I think, maybe you'd better tell me what it *is*." Her clear, steady voice projected an inner strength he hadn't noticed before.

"We weren't, uh, aren't...in love," he blurted with more emphasis than he'd intended.

She blinked again, but didn't move. He wished he could guess what she was thinking behind those wide eyes the color of summer leaves.

He tried to explain. "I didn't want you to expect—"

He hit a dead end. How could he renounce caring for her when his rebellious heart contradicted him with every beat? But such attraction was ridiculous. A grown man didn't fall head over heels for a stranger, no matter how perfect. Rachel O'Riley had cast a spell that had to be broken. Otherwise, his well-laid plans were ruined.

"What I mean," he chose his words carefully, "is

that sometimes people *do* fall in love just by ex-
changing letters, but…''

Her feathery eyebrows peaked, laughter sparked
in her eyes and she blinked again. She seemed to be
enjoying his discomfort.

Her amusement goaded him to be more blunt than
he'd planned. ''Anyway, I don't love you.''

There, he'd said it.

When he looked at her, he wished he'd cut out
his tongue before uttering the words. Her lower lip
trembled, tears filled her eyes and her shoulders
shook. For a horrible instant, he feared she would
break into sobs.

Then, as if she could contain herself no longer,
she burst out laughing.

He shoved his chair away from the bed and stood,
scratching his head at her reaction. Maybe the knock
on her head had caused more problems than amnesia.

''That,'' she gasped, ''is the most unromantic
proposal I hope I'll *ever* receive. If it was that awful
the first time, I must have been crazy to accept. It's
probably best I *can't* remember.''

She wiped her eyes with a corner of the sheet and
stared at him, her lips twitching as if she wanted to
laugh again.

He stuffed his hands in the back pockets of his
jeans and gazed out the window to avoid her ironic
smile. He should be happy she wasn't taking his
proposal too seriously, but her amusement annoyed
him. ''Maybe talking about this should wait until
your memory returns.''

''No, please.''

He whirled back toward her at the panic in her voice. "But without all the details, it sounds so..."

"Cold?"

He nodded. He hadn't had a problem with their agreement before, but now, seeing her so fragile that a puff of wind could blow her away, staring at him from the hospital bed with those big eyes...

"Maybe you'd better tell me all the details," she suggested in a calmer voice.

"The nurse wants you to rest."

He needed time to think, to figure out the best way to explain. Time to cool his simmering desire, brought about, he assured himself, only by the intimacy of the hospital room and her scanty attire. He barely knew the woman. How could he be attracted to her?

"I'll rest better once you've told me everything." Her guileless expression pleaded with him. "If I know the facts, my imagination won't exaggerate things."

He couldn't understand his reluctance. She'd known all the particulars before her accident and had agreed to the arrangement. Why should stating them a second time make any difference?

Because she's not just words on a page anymore. She's a real person, flesh and blood with feelings, who makes me feel alive again for the first time in years.

"Okay," he said with a sigh of resignation, "I'll try to explain."

He opened his mouth, but again words failed him. He'd never felt this stupid before. If she'd been a lame horse or an ailing cow, a broken chainsaw or a clogged pump, he'd know exactly what to do, but she was a woman, a beautiful and charming female, and he had almost no experience to fall back on. What little know-how he'd once possessed was rusty from lack of practice.

"Maybe," she suggested gently, "you should start at the beginning."

In the beginning there was Maggie, he thought.

"I was married before," Wade said.

Chapter Three

Rachel tamped down her rising panic. What had she gotten herself into, agreeing to marry a man she didn't know, a man whose first marriage had obviously ended in divorce?

Out of nowhere, a visceral reluctance to commit herself to any man bore down, engulfed her, then vanished as quickly as mist on the river evaporated in the sunlight. The irrational sensation made her fear the wreck had affected more than her memory.

Maybe she was losing her mind.

Or maybe Wade Garrett's faltering revelation had induced her fleeting dread of intimacy.

He was taking his sweet time explaining their so-called engagement, but she wouldn't pressure him. She wasn't going anywhere, not anytime soon. And if his details were as disastrous as his proposal, maybe she had better absorb them slowly.

Clearing her face of any reaction, she waited.

"My wife, Maggie, died in childbirth six years ago."

"I'm sorry," she said with sincerity, feeling stupid for jumping to conclusions about divorce.

His face had hardened when he spoke his wife's name. Rachel swallowed hard. She remembered nothing about herself or her past, but at that instant, more than anything in the world, she hoped Wade Garrett would never look like that at the mention of her name.

His antagonism toward his wife, inscribed all over his handsome face, went a long way toward communicating why he had proposed to a woman he didn't love. Maybe he'd married Maggie, expecting happily ever after, and when it hadn't worked out that way, decided marriage wasn't for him.

But why had the-Rachel-she-couldn't-remember agreed to a loveless marriage? She wouldn't know the answer until her memories returned.

Unless Wade could tell her.

"My son, Jordan, is eight now." Affection mixed with frustration glimmered in his deep brown eyes.

An intriguing image of Wade as husband and father flitted through her mind. "It must have been tough, raising a child alone all those years."

He settled back on his chair. "Ursula did most of the raising."

"Ursula?"

"Ursula's my housekeeper," he said, "and she's done a good job with Jordan. But now her arthritis is so bad, she can't keep up with the little rascal."

Comprehension flooded through her, leaving disappointment in its wake. "So that's why you need a wife. To take care of Jordan."

He nodded and relaxed. "I knew you'd understand. You did before when we discussed this in our letters."

Letters. He'd already told her they'd never met. "Why did you choose *me* to write to?"

He leaned forward and rested his strong chin with its charming cleft on his forearms, crossed on the back of the chair. His tanned face beamed with enthusiasm. "Your letter was hands down the best answer to my ad."

"I answered an *ad?*" She failed to keep the horror from her voice. What kind of woman was she to have answered a personal ad from a stranger?

Desperate?

Lonely?

Crazy?

All of the above?

"I saved your letters," he said. "If you want, I'll bring them next time I visit."

She struggled to dredge up lost memories, but the vast hole where her recollections should have been yielded nothing. "What did I say in my letters?"

"You described how much you'd enjoyed growing up on a farm."

"I lived on a farm?" The concept seemed so alien, she shuddered. Whatever trauma she had suffered had erased her memories so completely that she couldn't imagine farm life, much less remember it.

"Until four years ago."

Without evidence to contradict him, she'd have to take his word. "Anything else?"

"Your experience with country life is important, considering the way I live."

What kind of life had she agreed to? "You're a farmer?"

He frowned at the label. "No."

"Then why is my farm experience important?"

"I'm a rancher. I raise cattle and timber."

Nothing he said rang any bells, and her head swam with efforts to remember. A single mystery looming in her mind distressed her most. "Did I explain in my letters why I was willing to marry a perfect stranger and care for his child without—"

She floundered, searching for the right word.

Wade was no help. He just sat there, staring at her with amusement sparkling in his eyes. Again he reminded her of the Marlboro Man. A tall, rugged, sexy outdoorsman about as anxious to commit to love as a tumbleweed.

"Without..." She groped for a suitable phrase, bewailing silently that she'd lost not only her memories but her vocabulary, too.

"Without sex?" he suggested.

"That's not what I meant." Embarrassment scorched her face, and with relief, she latched on to the words she'd been searching for. "Without all the advantages of marriage. That's what I was trying to say."

He lifted his right brow and considered her with a grin. "You don't think sex is an advantage of marriage?"

"No." Memories, hovering at the edge of her consciousness, contradicted her.

"No?" Wade's raised brows registered his surprise.

The memory faded. "I mean yes, but I was talking about love, affection, mutual respect...." She widened her eyes as a possibility hit her. "Sex wasn't part of our agreement, was it?"

He straightened in his chair, and his teasing expression sobered. "Our agreement is purely business. You take care of Jordan and help run the house and ranch. In return, you have your own room, all expenses paid, and you receive a percentage of the yearly profits. When Jordan reaches adulthood, you can have a divorce, no questions asked."

She collapsed against her pillows, shocked to learn she'd agreed to such a sad, barren life. As for Wade, his cold, unsentimental terms clashed with his warm personality, and she wondered what had driven him to demand such an impersonal arrangement.

"Why go through the motions of getting married?" she said. "Why not just hire another housekeeper?"

He tunneled his fingers through his thick hair, a gesture she'd come to associate with him, and clasped his hands behind his head. The movement stretched his denim shirt across well-developed chest muscles. Wade Garrett was a good-looking, agreeable man who probably had hordes of local single women beating down his door. Why hadn't he married one of them?

"Longhorn Lake is a small community," he said. "A young housekeeper couldn't live at the ranch without causing a scandal."

"Then hire an older woman."

He dropped his hands to his knees and shook his head. "Jordan needs a mother, a real mother—"

"A real mother is the woman his father loves, not a business partner."

Wade avoided her gaze. "I don't intend to fall in love. And I can't marry anyone from the community."

"Why not?"

"Maggie's memory," he said cryptically.

She rubbed her throbbing temples with her fingertips to try to ease her pain and confusion. "I don't understand."

He scooted from his chair to the bed, pulled her back against his chest and began massaging her forehead. "I'd rather not talk about Maggie," he said in a flat tone.

She would have pushed him further, but the lazy circles of his fingers against her temples, the comforting pressure of his chest against her back and the warmth of his breath against her neck distracted her and caused the discontent constantly hovering inside to dwindle for the first time since she'd regained consciousness.

She had never felt so safe in a man's arms.

Wade's fingers stalled in their circling, and he dropped his hands to her shoulders. "Jordan needs a woman who'll be a permanent fixture in his life, someone he can be proud of. Someone he can introduce at school and church as his mom, so he'll be like the other kids and maybe stop—" He halted abruptly, as if he'd said too much.

So Jordan had some kind of problem, and Wade wanted a ready-made mother to deal with him. "How can you be sure Jordan will like me?"

His fingers, toying with a curl of her hair, brushed

the sensitive skin of her ear, transmitting dangerous flutters down her spine.

"You love children," he explained, as if that fact transcended all difficulties. "You said so in your letters."

What had she gotten herself into? She had problems enough already. No memory. No family. No money. And no idea how long she'd be confined to this hospital bed.

Just thinking about her troubles exhausted her. She sagged against Wade's chest and closed her eyes.

"I'm a stupid fool," Wade said with a growl.

She opened her eyes and forced a weak smile, but her weariness prevented further movement. "From the arrangement you've described, I tend to agree with you."

"I meant—" he stood up, laid her back on her pillow and leaned with one hand on each side of her, his face hovering inches from hers "—I'm a stupid fool to keep you talking when you should be sleeping."

She inhaled the pleasing scent of leather, soap and sunshine, and gazed into genial brown eyes flecked with gold. The closeness of his deeply tanned face with its sweep of dark lashes and appealing smile made her skin hot.

"I wanted answers to my questions," she said.

"No more questions now. You need to rest. Sweet dreams, Rachel. I'll stop in tomorrow. Maybe all those memories will have flooded back by then."

He patted her cheek with a warm, callused hand, then settled his battered Stetson low on his forehead.

At the door, he turned and touched his fingers to the brim of his hat, looking for all the world like a Western movie hero. When he disappeared into the hall, her hospital room seemed empty and cold.

She drifted into a twilight slumber between consciousness and sleep, only to wake with a jolt.

Wade hadn't answered her most important question: why *she* had agreed to a marriage without love.

TEN DAYS LATER, although Wade had visited her every day, she hadn't found the courage to ask the question again. She had hoped for a rapid return of her memories, and with them, her rationale for accepting Wade's unusual marriage proposal, but her past remained a frustrating blank. With her future and all its uncertainties a gaping void, she clung now to the one solid and steadfast element of her present.

Wade Garrett.

The day of her release had arrived, and she thanked the nurses and Dr. Sinclair for their care. Happy to have exchanged the shapeless hospital gown for jeans, a T-shirt and sneakers the nurse said were hers, she waited for Wade in her hospital room.

A half hour later, Rachel left the hospital and walked at Wade's side across the asphalt parking lot beneath the sweeping dome of Montana's big sky.

As they headed west in his pickup along Highway 2, she gazed at his tanned profile, partially obscured by the brim of his Stetson and his mirrored sunglasses. She wondered if he'd sent a picture with his letters, and if the-Rachel-she-couldn't-remember had fallen hopelessly in love with his sturdy good looks, in spite of his insistence on a strictly business liaison.

No wonder she'd said yes in her letters. Handsome, considerate, good-humored and stable, Wade embodied all the traits of the perfect husband.

Except he didn't love her. He'd made that crystal clear.

Unable to remember why she'd agreed to marry him in the first place, she struggled now with whether to go through with his bizarre marriage proposal.

She hoped she wouldn't regret accepting his invitation to stay at his ranch, but, broke and remembering no one, she had nowhere else to go. According to Wade, the authorities reported she had closed her bank account and canceled her credit cards before leaving Atlanta. If she'd had any money, it had disappeared. Her wallet was empty of everything but her ID card and a paper with Wade's name and address, the information that had caused the local sheriff to summon Wade to her bedside.

"Thanks for offering me a place to stay."

"No problem." His agreeable smile hit her with the scorching intensity of the noonday sun. "It was the least I could do, since you gave up your apartment and job in Atlanta to marry me."

Just the thought of marriage to the mesmerizing rancher created an erratic quiver in her stomach. "You promised—"

"I know," he said with another heart-stopping smile, "no mention of marriage until you're ready to discuss it."

She reclined against the seat and barely registered

the unfamiliar landscape flashing by. Her traitorous
mind refused to yield its captive memories, swelling
instead with seductive images of life as Mrs. Wade
Garrett. She had extracted Wade's promise of silence on the subject of matrimony, not because the
prospect was distasteful but because of its disturbing
attractiveness.

Twenty minutes out of Libby, Wade turned off
the highway, which paralleled a river road signs
identified as the Kootenai, swollen now with melting
snow, onto a blacktop road that cut straight through
a broad, green valley nestled between two majestic
mountain ranges.

"We call this God's country," he said. "Bet
you've never seen this part of Montana before."

She laughed with bittersweet humor. "That's a
safe bet. Even if I had, I wouldn't remember."

On the narrow, two-lane road, they traveled past
broad pastures where cattle grazed, and sped through
intermittent stands of cedars and pines. A cloudless
sky of vivid blue arched above the endless miles.

She rolled down her window and inhaled the fragrance of warm grasses and invigorating pine. "It's
good to breathe fresh air instead of the smell of an-
tiseptic."

"You're an outdoor girl. Maybe," he said with
rough gentleness as he slowed the truck, "living on
the ranch will jar your memories loose."

"Maybe."

Wade lifted his hand from the wheel and gave
hers an encouraging squeeze. "You mustn't worry.
Everything's going to be fine."

His touch cheered her. With hope, she clung to

the expectation that her past would soon be restored, and rejected the possibility of her memory loss being permanent. Dr. Sinclair had advised her not to worry about her amnesia, but to take one day at a time.

Wade turned off the blacktop and drove beneath an arched sign of rough-hewn timber with Longhorn Valley Ranch burned into the wood in tall, rustic letters.

His face lit with pride as he pointed west across a wide pasture edged on the far side by a curving line of trees. "The river runs through our property there. The Garretts have owned these grazing lands and forests for over a century."

She envied his heritage, stretching back a hundred years. He belonged to the land. She could hear the attachment in his voice, see it in his eyes.

She belonged nowhere.

The truck had proceeded only a hundred yards between the ancient cedars that lined the drive when the acrid stench of smoke filled the cab.

She wrinkled her nose. "What's burning?"

Wade slammed on the brakes, swung out of the truck and lifted his face to the wind. Blowing out of the east, the breeze reeked of burning wood.

"There." He indicated smoke rising from a stand of mature trees.

"A forest fire. On your land?"

He nodded and his mouth hardened into a grim line. "My best timber, ready for harvest."

He leaped back into the truck and, with a grinding of gears, floored the accelerator. She braced against the door as the truck bounced along the miles of dirt track beneath the trees. Within a few minutes, the road ended in a circular drive in front of a large house, and the pickup screeched to a halt.

Two sprawling stories made of weathered logs, with a wide porch shaded by rambler roses heavy with crimson blooms, the century-old house sat between two gigantic ponderosa pines. Although Wade had said she'd never visited his ranch before, she experienced an illogical sensation of coming home.

Her rush of pleasure at the sight of the stalwart but gracious house was interrupted by the shout of a tiny woman, white haired and frail, who waited on the front porch, her hands wrapped in her apron. "Wade Garrett, you came up that drive like a bat outta hell. Ain't no sense in getting yourself killed over a little fire."

Wade wrenched open the door and jumped from the truck. "A *little* fire! It's dry season, Ursula, and the wind's blowing! The whole mountain could go up in flames."

"No need to panic." Ursula appeared unruffled by Wade's outburst. "The Forest Service and volunteers already have everything under control. I'm fixing to feed 'em supper soon as they finish mopping up."

Rachel climbed down from the cab. "If you're expecting a crowd, may I help?"

She'd taken a chance, asking. She didn't remember if she could cook, but memories weren't required to wash dishes.

Ursula's smile subtracted years from her weathered face, and she extended a gnarled hand. "You must be Rachel. Thanks for offering."

The old woman's demeanor conveyed not only

welcome but acceptance, and as Rachel shook her hand, she experienced again an impression of home-coming.

Wade pivoted and headed back to his truck. "I'd better see if they need help."

"You got more important work—" Ursula jerked her thumb toward the house "—upstairs."

Wade turned. "Jordan? Is he hurt?"

Rachel registered a shock of empathy at the fear and concern on Wade's face.

"No," Ursula said, "but he's in his room, crying his eyes out, afraid you'll tan his hide good this time."

"You know I've never laid a hand on..." He glanced toward the smoking pines. "Jordan started the fire?"

Feeling like an intruder, Rachel retreated into the shade of the porch, but she couldn't avoid the argument between Wade and his housekeeper.

"Don't be too hard on the boy," Ursula said. "He was just trying to please you."

"By burning down my best timber? I'll—"

"Wade Garrett!" Ursula drilled him with a scowl. "For the past twenty years, you've been like a son to me, but if you don't start giving that boy what he needs, I swear, I'll disown you."

Wade yanked off his hat, slapped it against his thigh and pointed at Rachel. "I've brought him what he needs. A mother."

Rachel flinched as the full impact of mail-order bride status hit her. Wade had treated her with no more respect than some fourth-class package.

Ursula stepped toward Wade and shook her finger

at him. "Sometimes I think you couldn't pour water out of a boot with instructions on the heel—"

"Tell Jordan I'll talk to him at supper." Wade crushed his hat back on and strode to the truck. With a ferocious grinding of gears, he peeled off in a flurry of dust.

Ursula climbed the porch steps as if her arthritis pained her, and approached Rachel. "Thank God, you're here, girl. Don't mind Wade's rough ways. He's all heart underneath his bluster. But both Wade and Jordan, they need you more than you could ever imagine."

Rachel watched the haze of dust that marked Wade's progress toward the fire. She didn't doubt his love for Jordan. In the surprising outburst from the man who had impressed her with his even-tempered nature, she had recognized his frustration over Jordan's mischief.

Most telling of all, Wade obviously believed all his boy needed to cure his troubles was a mother.

Rachel wasn't so sure. After all, she wasn't the boy's mother, but a total stranger. Not the woman his father loved, only someone who had responded to a personal ad. And any skills or experience she might once have used to benefit a troubled boy lay buried deep in her damaged psyche.

With a sinking sensation that she'd stumbled into more than she could handle, Rachel followed Ursula into the house.

Chapter Four

Rachel accompanied Ursula through the broad central hall of the house. Doors to adjoining rooms opened on either side, and a wide staircase rose to the second floor, but she paid little attention to her surroundings, beyond the walls' chinked-log construction, polished hardwood floors, spaciousness created by high ceilings, and the tantalizing aroma of cinnamon in the air.

Ursula stepped through a door at the end of the hall and preceded Rachel into a bright, oversize kitchen. Cheery yellow-checkered curtains flanked the ample windows, and a monstrous, black wood-burning stove with logs stacked beside it dominated one end of the room.

The logs reminded Rachel of Wade's timber. "The forest fire—did it do much damage?"

From a hook behind the door, Ursula removed a gingham apron, a twin to the one she wore, and handed it to Rachel. Her pleasant features darkened. "Enough to take a bite out of Wade's timber profits this year."

"I'm sorry."

Rachel recalled the agony on Wade's face when he realized the blaze was on his land. After the kindness he had shown her, losing his timber didn't seem fair.

The housekeeper gave her a peeler and indicated a small mountain of potatoes on the well-scrubbed wooden table. "Wade planned to use the money from that timber to buy more land this year."

"Can't he use the income from his cattle?" As Rachel hefted a potato and fumbled with the unfamiliar feel of the peeler, the rudeness of her question struck her. "Sorry, it's really none of my—"

"Course it's your business. You're going to be his partner, aren't you?"

"Maybe." She glanced at her hands to conceal her blushing and avoid the housekeeper's probing look.

"Cattle business ain't what it used to be," Ursula grumbled as she filled a pot the size of a washtub with water and set it on the massive stove, "but Wade's better at raising beef than anyone else in this part of the state."

If Rachel entertained the slightest inclination toward accepting Wade's strange proposal, she'd need all the information she could gather. Encouraged by Ursula's openness, she posed another question. "Doesn't it take a lot of money to operate a huge ranch like this?"

Ursula picked up a paring knife and attacked the skin of a potato. "Wade's a good manager. When cattle prices are up, he sets something aside for leaner years. His timber's always been icing on the cake. Investing the money from those sales has made him the wealthiest man in the valley.''

Ursula had already peeled two potatoes to Rachel's one, assaulting the spuds as if they were enemies. Rachel marveled at the swiftness of the weathered hands, misshapen by arthritis. If Wade expected her to replace this paragon of domesticity, she had a lot to learn.

''This year's timber's gone,'' Ursula said, ''but because of Wade's investments, he won't ever have to break the promise he made his daddy.''

''What promise was that?'' Rachel wiped the finger she'd nicked with the peeler on her apron.

''Never to sell off part of Longhorn Valley Ranch. A real estate agent from Great Falls has been hovering around here like a buzzard, offering to buy the land along the river for an outrageous price.''

''If the ranch's profits are variable, why would someone else offer outrageous money for just a strip of it?''

''The Realtor wants to subdivide it into 'estates' for all them wealthy folks moving from California to escape crime.'' Ursula spoke as if the words left a bad taste in her mouth.

Rachel shrugged. ''If the land's standing empty, why doesn't Wade sell and invest the profit?''

''You got a lot to learn about Wade Garrett, girl. He *never* breaks a promise.'' Ursula laughed with sardonic humor. ''You got a lot to learn about working a ranch, too. If he sold that land, he'd lose his water rights.''

Rachel glanced at the faucets on the sink. ''But you have water.''

"Without the river, Wade couldn't water his cattle or the tree seedlings he'll be planting soon. So without the river frontage, he might as well sell the whole kit and caboodle."

"Is Dad gonna sell the ranch?" a high, thin voice behind Ursula asked. "It's my fault, isn't it?"

Ursula swiveled in her chair, allowing Rachel a view of a small boy standing in the doorway, his eyes red and swollen and his sooty cheeks tracked with tears. Even if she hadn't known who he was, she would have recognized Jordan as a startling miniature of his father, less muscular and self-assured, but with the same heart-stopping good looks that would one day drive women wild.

For now, he was a very frightened and unhappy little boy. Despite her act of bravado over her lost memory, Rachel knew exactly how he felt.

"Come in and meet Rachel," Ursula said.

The boy hunched his thin shoulder to wipe his face on the sleeve of his T-shirt, and approached Rachel as if he had lead in his sneakers. The loneliness in his big brown eyes stabbed at her heart and mirrored her own.

"Hello, Jordan. Your daddy's told me lots about you."

"He did?" His gamin face brightened at the mention of Wade.

"You bet," Rachel said. "From what I can tell, you're the most important person in your daddy's whole world."

A transforming smile filled with the innocence and hope of childhood swept across his face before the sadness returned. "Not anymore. Not after to-day."

"Everybody makes mistakes, Jordan. Even if your father is angry at what you've done, he still loves you." Rachel reached out and grasped his shoulders lightly.

For one small instant, the boy looked as if he'd like to throw himself into her arms. Then his expression hardened, and he jerked from her grasp. "He just wants me to stay out of trouble and out of his way."

Across the table, Ursula raised her eyebrows and flashed Rachel a knowing look that said, *See what you're in for?*

Rachel understood loneliness and fear. She'd had her fill of both the last two weeks. But she was an adult and, even without memories, more equipped to deal with life than this small boy, trying so hard to be brave. Her heart ached for him.

He headed toward the door, then turned back with a suspicious glare. "Are you going to live here?"

"I don't know." She told the truth, not only because he deserved it, but because he'd know if she lied. "I haven't decided yet."

"Guess you don't want to be around a kid who causes so much trouble." His narrowed eyes and the aggressive jut of his chin dared her to disagree.

She rose to the bait with honesty. "If I *do* stay, you'll be the main reason."

"Me?" Astonishment replaced his pugnacious look.

"You." The smile of warmth and approval she

gave him originated deep inside. "I think I'm going to like you very much."

Grinning as if she'd given him a priceless gift, Jordan turned and rushed out the door.

A FEW HOURS LATER, with Band-Aids plastered on her cuts from the potato peeler, Rachel crossed the grassy back lawn and followed a dirt track toward the barn. The Forest Service firefighters and volunteers had already gathered at makeshift picnic tables on the side lawn and helped themselves to Ursula's grilled steaks, mashed potatoes and fresh-picked salad. When she and Ursula had served the apple pies and Wade still hadn't appeared, Rachel had gone in search of him.

She found him at a large washtub beside the barn, stripped to the waist.

He dunked his head into the water just as she approached, and the broad, smooth muscles of his back glinted golden in the last rays of the sun as it dropped behind the mountains. He pulled his head from the water and whipped his streaming hair back from his face, radiating strength and virility like the sun projects light.

At the sight of him, she wondered anew why every unattached female in the county wasn't set on marrying him. He'd said he wouldn't marry a local girl because of Maggie's memory, but had refused to elaborate. His unspoken anger at the mention of Maggie's name suggested his reluctance had nothing to do with honoring Maggie's memory. But what else it could be was a mystery. If Wade wouldn't tell her, maybe Ursula would.

Still, it was a shame some woman couldn't wake up every morning to those seductive brown eyes, closed now as he groped along the bench beside the tub for his towel.

She scurried forward and grabbed the cloth, which had fallen into the dirt. Flicking it clean, she thrust it into his hands. He dried his face before opening his eyes.

"Thanks." He toweled his hair, seeming unsurprised to find her there.

She averted her eyes from his bare chest and muscled arms and gazed instead over the adjacent field of tall grass that stretched toward the river. But looking away didn't prevent the scent of spicy soap and a faint whiff of wood smoke from reminding her of his presence.

His deal with her was only business, she reminded her mutinous senses.

"You had supper?" he asked.

"The others are almost finished, but I was waiting for you."

"Why?"

At the surprise in his tone, she wheeled to face him. "I want to talk to you about Jordan."

He shrugged into a clean denim shirt and began fastening the buttons. "What about him?"

She'd spent a half hour with the boy while he picked at his supper and cast anxious glances toward the barn in anticipation of his father's return. "He's scared to death."

Finished with his buttons, Wade turned his back, a small concession to modesty, unzipped his jeans and tucked in his shirt. The intimacy of standing with a man she barely knew as he bathed and dressed in the gathering twilight would have unnerved her more if she hadn't been so concerned for the boy.

He zipped his jeans and swiveled to face her. "Jordan doesn't have anything to be scared of."

She wanted to shake Wade as, without a clue to his son's torment, he calmly rolled up his sleeves. "He's scared to death of *you*."

He flinched as if she'd struck him. "Me? That's ridiculous."

"Is it?" She had learned a lot from the boy in her short interval with him. "When did you last spend any time with him?"

"I can't be everywhere. I've been at the hospital with you for almost two weeks."

Lucky for him, a trace of guilt filtered through the defensiveness in his voice, or her anger would have exploded. "And before that?"

He stopped and thought. "Week before last, when final report cards came out. I set him straight about his C in language arts."

"What were his other grades?"

He shrugged. "A's and B's."

Common sense told her to back off from the man who was offering her the hospitality of his home, but the terror she'd witnessed in Jordan's face prodded her on. "What did you say about his good grades?"

He combed his damp hair with his fingers. "What was there to say? They were fine."

When he set off toward the house, she took three strides to his one to keep pace. "Wade Garrett, if you want me to honor the promise I made before my accident, you'd better stop right now and hear me out.''

"We're not married yet, Rachel girl.'' He stopped and faced her. A muscle twitched at the corner of his mouth in an insinuation of a grin. "It's a little early for you to start bossing me around.''

"Bossing…?'' She held her breath and counted silently to ten while he stared with a provocative half smile on his too-darned-handsome face. She exhaled, calmer, and broached the reason for her confrontation. "Jordan's terrified you'll punish him for starting the fire.''

A rock-hard grimness replaced the half smile. "He *should* be punished.''

Her stomach churned with frustration. "Punished for trying to get his daddy's attention by doing something you'd be proud of?''

The harsh line of his mouth remained taut. "I don't recall anybody handing out prizes to firebugs. The boy's got to learn the difference between right and wrong.''

"He *knows* the difference. What Jordan needs to learn is that his father *loves* him.'' If Wade hadn't been so huge, with a build like a boulder, she'd have jostled him till his teeth rattled. "He didn't set that fire on purpose. You should know him better than that.''

Wade lifted one dark eyebrow in question, but his mouth remained stern.

Undeterred, Rachel plowed ahead. "From the short time I've been around him, I can tell Jordan's not a troublemaker.''

"He could've fooled me." Wade lowered his face to within inches of hers and heaved a frustrated sigh. "I could make a list as long as my arm of the trouble that kid's been in, just in the last month."

She crossed her arms over her chest and glared. "And it never occurred to you to wonder why?"

"Because he doesn't have a mother to keep him in line, that's why. That's where you come in." His slow grin sent shivers of delight coursing down her back.

But she refused to be distracted. "Jordan wants *you* to notice him."

Wade regarded her with a look half quizzical, half amused. "What are you, a psychologist?"

She gritted her teeth. "It doesn't take a psychologist, or a rocket scientist, to see Jordan needs your attention. Today he was trying, all by himself, to fulfill the requirements for a camping award."

"What?" At least Wade had the grace to look bewildered.

"You didn't know he was working on the project?"

He flung his arms wide and rolled his eyes. "That's Ursula's job."

Her temper rising, Rachel scowled. "Your attitude explains why the poor kid's been struggling on his own to master camping skills."

"A camping award isn't worth burning down my timber," Wade said, but he sounded less sure of himself than before.

"He didn't intend to burn your timber! He was teaching himself to start a fire without matches."

Wade massaged the back of his neck as if he had

a pain. "Judging from ten acres of ashes, I'd say he's mastered the technique."

Rachel rammed her fists on her hips and lifted her chin to meet Wade's mellow gaze. "The wind picked up and blew sparks into dry grass. Jordan tried to stomp it out. When that didn't work, he attempted to beat it out with his shirt. You're lucky your son wasn't burned alive trying to save your precious timber."

Wade shook his head in disbelief. "All over a camping award?"

"Didn't you hear what I just said? Your son could have been burned to a crisp, a part of those ashes you're complaining about."

For a moment, when his assured expression slipped and doubt glinted in his eyes, she thought she'd made her point.

Then he broke into a grin. "Now that you're here, you can keep him safe."

"Aargh!"

Rachel wheeled and hurried toward the house, leaving him alone in the driveway. She shouldn't have bothered explaining. Despite the compassion Wade had shown her after the train wreck, he was as ignorant as a mule where Jordan was concerned.

Recalling the boy's tear-streaked face, Rachel whirled and returned to Wade.

"Why can't you get it through your thick head it's his father's approval, not some award, that's important to Jordan?" She poked her finger against the hard muscles of his chest. "The poor kid believes he has to win a medal, just so his own father will love him."

She snatched her finger away and clenched her trembling hands at her side, astonished by the strong maternal urge that had overwhelmed her, infusing her with an unfamiliar courage. Either some repressed memory had activated her response, or the skinny little kid had worked some kind of spell on her.

A glance at Wade made her rethink her last assumption. His eyes, alight with growing awareness, gleamed in the twilight like polished stones. She squirmed beneath his rapt gaze.

Maybe it wasn't Jordan who had cast a spell.

Horrified at her boldness, she raced across the dew-wet grass toward the house, fleeing Wade's probing scrutiny and the corresponding quiver in her heart.

WADE WATCHED HER GO. He'd wanted a mother for Jordan, so why wasn't he delighted when Rachel acted like one?

Because she's pointing out your faults.

He ignored the twinge of conscience. He'd done his best with Jordan, raising the boy as his own dad had raised him, with an iron hand, strict rules and swift and speedy punishment for misbehavior. And he, Wade, had turned out all right, hadn't he? True, he'd always had more fear than fondness for his father, but the ornery old cuss had taught him right from wrong and how to run a ranch. Passing on those values was more important than love, wasn't it?

Besides, Wade had to instill in Jordan a strong

moral fiber, so he wouldn't grow up to be like his mother.

The memory of Rachel's green eyes reproached him, and he attempted to relieve his guilty conscience with more excuses, but he was too bone-tired to argue, even with himself. He'd spent hours helping the firefighters hose down hot spots. All he wanted now was a hot meal and a good night's sleep.

If that blur of dust coming up the drive from the highway was what he suspected, he wouldn't enjoy either anytime soon. With regret, he ambled to the front of the house and waited on the porch as the vehicle approached.

A midnight-blue Mercedes halted in the circular drive behind the line of green Forest Service vehicles with their distinctive yellow shields.

A tall, blond man, about his own age and dressed in an expensive dark suit with silk tie, French cuffs and tasseled loafers, climbed out and advanced toward the porch.

"I'm looking for Wade Garrett," he said.

Another blasted real estate agent. This one hadn't even waited for the smoke to clear before swooping down like a vulture after roadkill.

Wade reined in his temper. "That's me. Who are you?"

The stranger offered his hand. His lips smiled, but his blue eyes were cold. "Larry Crutchfield. Dr. Sinclair told me where to reach you."

When he realized Crutchfield was no Realtor, Wade squinted in confusion. "What's this all about?"

"Rachel O'Riley. I've followed her all the way from Atlanta."

A black cloud of foreboding settled over Wade, but he invited the man inside. As they crossed the porch, voices drifted from the side yard, where the firefighters lingered after supper.

"I'm not interrupting a party or something?" Crutchfield asked.

"Not exactly." Wade preceded his guest into the hall and opened the door to the living room. "Have a seat."

Crutchfield sat on the sofa, looking ready to bolt. Something was making his guest mighty antsy, and Wade, guessing that something had to do with Rachel, felt his own nerves tighten. "You're here about Rachel?"

"Is she here? Is she all right?"

"Why don't you answer my questions first, seeing as how you're sitting in my house."

Crutchfield nodded. "I'm an attorney."

Wade's eyebrows rose. "Rachel isn't in trouble with the law?"

"No." Crutchfield's smile was warmer this time, but the pleasant expression did little to ease Wade's wariness. "She was a paralegal with my firm before she quit a few weeks ago."

"Maybe you could get to the point," Wade said. "I take it you're not here to deliver severance pay."

Crutchfield cleared his throat with a nervous cough. "I'm here to take Rachel home with me."

Crutchfield's announcement caught Wade by surprise. He narrowed his eyes, considering his visitor in a new light, and a fierce protectiveness toward

Rachel swelled inside him. "Why should Rachel go home with you?"

The lawyer smiled with disturbing self-assurance. "Rachel is my fiancée. We're supposed to be married next month."

Wade sank into the nearest chair. Rachel had never mentioned Crutchfield in her letters. If she really was engaged to someone else, that fact grieved him more than he was willing to admit. But the inconvenience of finding another wife wasn't what distressed him. Since she'd regained consciousness after the accident, she'd made his life a lot more interesting. In those few short days, he'd taken for granted her sunny smile and pleasant laugh.

He was reluctant to lose her now, and vowed silently not to let her go. Not unless her memories returned and she convinced him she wanted to. Maybe a breakup with Crutchfield had prompted Rachel to answer Wade's ad. If she'd agreed to marry Wade because Crutchfield had rejected her, or she'd decided to leave him, Wade would be damned if he'd just hand her over to the attorney.

And what about Jordan? Who else would care so much so quickly about his son?

Maybe you should let her go, an inner voice warned. *You once loved Maggie, and she brought you nothing but grief.*

But this was different. He didn't *love* Rachel, he argued with himself. He just liked having her around. For Jordan's sake.

"Dr. Sinclair explained about Rachel's amnesia," Crutchfield was saying. "She suggested I not tell Rachel who I am unless she recognizes me."

Wade clung to a small hope. "And if she doesn't?"

"I'll take it a day at a time, like the doctor suggested. I can find a place nearby so I'll be here when her memory returns."

With a sinking sensation in the pit of his stomach, Wade pushed himself to his feet. "There's only one way to find out if she remembers you. Come with me."

Wade led Crutchfield out the front door and around the side of the house. Someone had turned on the outdoor floodlights and lit citronella candles against insects. At the table nearest the kitchen, Rachel sat with Jordan, her head bowed, listening as he read from a book.

Crutchfield grabbed Wade's arm, and they paused in the shadows.

"What is it?" Wade asked.

Crutchfield nodded toward the crowd. "Where is she?"

"Don't you see her? She's at the back table with my son."

Wade's heart pounded in his throat. Jordan had taken to Rachel immediately. Wade was discovering he himself was more taken with her than he'd been willing to admit. And now they both might lose her to some legal eagle from Atlanta.

Crutchfield's gaze scanned the yard. "I see a woman in jeans and a T-shirt, but I don't see Rachel."

Exasperated, Wade called, "Rachel, someone's here to meet you."

She lifted her head and graced him with a smile

that pierced him with its sweetness. Or was she looking at Crutchfield? She tousled Jordan's hair, scooted away from the table and sauntered across the yard toward them.

"Now do you see her?" Wade asked, angry at Crutchfield's intrusion and the questions he raised.

"Is this some kind of joke?" Crutchfield said. "I've never seen that woman before. She's not Rachel O'Riley."

Chapter Five

Wade's first reaction was relief. Rachel wasn't Crutchfield's fiancée, and the attorney wouldn't be taking her back to Atlanta, even if her memories returned.

Then the ramifications hit him. If the woman who could make his heart stutter like he'd been kicked in the chest wasn't the Rachel O'Riley who'd answered his ad, who was she?

Worry gripped him in a choke hold. Maybe she was *already* married. His face must have mirrored his emotions. Rachel was watching him as she strode across the grass, and her welcoming smile wavered.

He leaned toward Crutchfield and whispered, "Let me handle this. Just follow my lead."

Wade threw his arm around her shoulder when she reached them. "Rachel, this is Larry Crutchfield."

Rachel's appraisal of Crutchfield took in his expensive suit and tie, which stuck out from the jeans and work shirts of Wade and the volunteers like a mule in a horse show. She offered her hand with a quizzical smile. ''Are you from the insurance company?''

Crutchfield's expression would have been funny under different circumstances, but Wade wasn't laughing. He latched on to Rachel's assumption. ''Right. He's a claims adjuster, here about the fire. We've got business to discuss.''

''But Jordan's waiting for you,'' Rachel said.

Feistiness heightened the color in her cheeks, reminding Wade of her spirited championing of his boy earlier. Obviously, she wasn't going to let him off the hook tonight without resolving Jordan's problem, but he could deal with only one crisis at a time.

''I won't be long.'' He grabbed Crutchfield's elbow, swung him back toward the house and lowered his voice. ''We need to talk, Crutchfield, but not here.''

He hurried the attorney toward the front of the house, while Rachel returned to Jordan.

''Where is *my* Rachel?'' Crutchfield demanded.

Wade took the porch steps three at a time and opened the screen door. ''Rachel O'Riley is your problem. *That* woman—'' he jerked his head toward the yard ''—is mine. She was brought into the county hospital after a train wreck, with Rachel O'Riley's identification card in her wallet. Because her memory's gone, she thinks she's Rachel. I did, too, until now.''

The lawyer resumed the seat he'd occupied earlier. ''How did she end up with you?''

''Wait here.'' Wade wheeled out of the room and sprinted upstairs, hoping the evidence he sought would prove Crutchfield wrong. He had only Crutchfield's word that the woman wasn't Rachel O'Riley. In the guest room, he retrieved Rachel's ID card with its dark undecipherable photograph before gathering her letters from his own room.

Crutchfield was pacing in front of the stone fireplace when Wade returned and handed him the ID. "Is this the Rachel O'Riley you're looking for?"

Crutchfield studied it, then removed a slim alligator wallet from his suit jacket and pulled out a picture. "This is Rachel."

Wade took the color studio portrait and crumpled into his chair. The female smiling up at him, although she had green eyes, held no other resemblance to the Rachel he knew, but the signature on the back of the picture was identical to the handwriting of his letters.

"That's Rachel O'Riley," Crutchfield said. "Not the woman outside."

"You're sure?"

"My fiancée doesn't even resemble this other woman," Crutchfield pointed out.

Wade agreed.

"Now will you tell me your connection with Rachel O'Riley?" Crutchfield said.

Wade felt a pang of sympathy for the attorney as he handed over Rachel's letters. Crutchfield scanned them hurriedly, then tossed them on the coffee table in disgust.

"This is all Aunt Myra's fault. She tried to convince me not to marry Rachel, said Rachel wasn't from a socially acceptable background. Her family were farmers, you know," he said with a hint of condescension. "But I was willing to marry her in spite of that."

Wade nodded, annoyed by Crutchfield's pretentious tone. "Does your fiancée know you're following her?"

"She spotted me in Chicago from the train window. I arrived just as it was leaving the station."

Wade wondered if the real Rachel O'Riley had fled because of Aunt Myra, or if she'd finally realized what a jerk her fiancée was.

"The real Rachel must have changed her mind about marrying me," Wade said, "and switched identities when…*my* Rachel lost consciousness in the accident."

Crutchfield's expression brightened. "So if I stay until your Rachel remembers who she is, I can track my fiancée using that name."

Wade drew himself to his full height, three inches taller than the lawyer. "Except you won't be hanging around here. That woman has suffered a terrible trauma. She believes she's Rachel O'Riley. If she discovers she's not before her memories start to return, her recovery could be set back, maybe forever. I can't risk having you around."

The lawyer regarded him with a dark glint of menace in his eyes. "You can't stop me."

Wade hooked his thumbs in his pockets and drilled his visitor with a frigid stare. "But the law can. I'll post No Trespassing signs, and if you come within a foot of that woman, I'll have you charged with harassment. Better yet, stalking."

"You forget you're dealing with a lawyer."

Wade's expression hardened. "And you'll be

dealing with me and Dan Howard, the sheriff of this county and my best friend. He and my ranch hands will make sure you leave us alone.''

Crutchfield's menacing look faded. ''I was planning to follow up on the train wreck anyway. Trace the whereabouts of the other female passengers.''

Wade shook his head at the attorney's failure to grasp the significance of his fiancée's disappearance. ''Why don't you go back to Atlanta? Rachel O'Riley doesn't want you. Why else would she have gone to so much trouble to disappear?''

Crutchfield's cocky expression returned. ''How could she *not* want to marry me? She just needed time to get her head straight.''

Wade held his temper and his tongue. Arguing with the arrogant Crutchfield was a waste of breath.

The attorney snatched up the color portrait, pivoted and left. Wade followed him to the front porch and watched him climb into his Mercedes and roar down the drive.

Larry Crutchfield was a sidewinder, for sure, and Wade would make certain the oily lawyer wouldn't come within a hundred feet of Rachel.

Wade returned to the living room and sank back into his chair. First thing tomorrow, he'd discuss this latest development with Dr. Sinclair and get her advice.

The screen door slammed, and he felt Rachel's presence in the room before he looked at her. Rachel—what else could he call her?—stood on the threshold, one slender hip propped against the door frame, an enigma in the flesh. And very appealing flesh, at that.

He quickly cataloged his scant knowledge of her. She possessed exceptional courage, evidenced by her acceptance of her amnesia without going to pieces. She obviously loved children, demonstrated by her willingness to confront him about Jordan. And an unnamed unhappiness often flickered briefly in the green abysses of her remarkable eyes.

Everything else—her name, where she came from, her past—was a mystery.

Suddenly an additional fact about the woman he'd asked to care for his son blindsided him with startling force. She made him feel alive again, for the first time since he had learned of Maggie's deception.

"Is Mr. Crutchfield going to pay the claim?" she asked.

Lost in contemplation, Wade frowned, then remembered he'd introduced his visitor as an adjuster. "He said he'll turn it over to his supervisor."

He grimaced at his lie. There was no insurance policy on the timber that had burned.

She smiled sympathetically, and her concern made his heart ache. She had problems of her own, but worried about him and his troubles. He hoisted himself to his feet.

They walked outside, and he shortened his stride to match hers. Her trusting glance as she slipped her arm through his, the warm pressure of her hand and the subtle floral fragrance of her soap filled him with peacefulness. Companionship and a mother for Jordan was all he really wanted, he assured himself. But *this* Rachel might be some other man's wife, some other child's mother.

He expanded the distance between them until she dropped her hand from his arm. He would have no true peace until he knew who she really was.

"You must be starving." Her musical voice blended with the rustle of the breeze and the faint hum of insects.

During the turmoil Crutchfield had created, Wade had forgotten supper, and learning the woman at his side wasn't Rachel O'Riley had stolen his appetite. But if he didn't eat, he'd tip off the observant not-Rachel that something was wrong.

He nodded toward the firefighters, still lingering over coffee. "Probably not much left after that hungry bunch finished."

"I fixed you a plate. Ursula's keeping it warm in the oven."

They approached the wooden table beneath the pines, and he caught sight of Jordan, his eyes round with apprehension, his too-thin face pale in the candlelight. The boy's obvious fear and unhappiness stabbed him with fresh worry.

"Hi, Dad." The boy's voice quivered.

Wade scooted onto the bench beside him and Rachel sat across the table, nodding encouragement to Jordan.

The boy looked at him and stiffened, as if preparing for the worst. "I'm sorry about your timber, Dad. I'll sell my pony to help pay for the damage."

Had his boy always been this terrified of him? Wade's anger at the boy's carelessness softened— until he recognized the ghost of the irresponsible Maggie in the boy's eyes.

Ursula's arrival interrupted Wade's thoughts. "Are you ready for your dinner?"

"Yes, thanks," he replied.

"Ursula," Rachel said, "how about another piece of pie for Jordan? He could use some fattening up."

"But he didn't finish his supper," Ursula argued.

"Please, just bring the pie—and put some ice cream on it," Rachel told her.

"Now, Jordan," Wade began.

When the already-rigid child tensed, Wade's exasperation increased. Why couldn't the boy take his punishment like a man? "Rachel explained how the fire started. You've been warned never to play with matches."

"I didn't use—"

"You know," Wade said, "that playing with fire in any form is dangerous and strictly forbidden. If it had been later in the dry season, thousands of acres could have burned."

Wade hesitated when Rachel's smooth forehead bunched in a frown, and she telegraphed her disapproval with a faint shake of her head, but he couldn't allow her to make a wimp of his son.

"Jordan," he said, "you're grounded for the next two weeks. I don't want you leaving the house unless an adult is with you. Do you understand?"

The boy nodded, his jaw quivering.

"I have to run some errands in town tomorrow," Wade continued, struck by an idea that would keep Jordan out of trouble and Rachel at Wade's side in case Crutchfield returned. "You and Rachel will come with me."

"Yes, sir." Jordan looked pleased, which surprised Wade. He'd viewed the order as punishment.

"Will you come?" he asked Rachel.

She nodded, her expression puzzled. Wade didn't blame her. He suddenly felt as if he'd lost control of the situation.

"Have you met Leo?" Wade asked, purposely changing subjects. Leo, Ursula's husband, had worked for Wade's father, and now, as ranch foreman, was the only hand who didn't sleep and eat in the bunkhouse beyond the barn.

Rachel nodded. "He had supper with us."

Wade stifled his reservations about neglecting the ranch for another morning. Leo had handled things fine the days Wade had spent at the hospital.

"Leo can take care of things here while we're in Libby," Wade said.

"And Jordan can show me the town," Rachel added.

Wade's gut lurched at Rachel's soft, maternal smile as she observed his son, and he grimaced inwardly at the irony of his situation. He had selected Rachel O'Riley because her letters, while warm and friendly, had failed to strike an emotional chord. If the real Rachel had appeared, their agreement probably would have been a genial but soulless one.

The baffling woman across from him was another matter entirely. She had reawakened long-slumbering emotions and stimulated others he hadn't known existed. How could such a woman *not* have someone who loved her, *not* have children of her own somewhere? Any minute now, another vehicle might roar up the drive, carrying a man to claim the woman whose name Wade didn't know.

He had to keep his distance. He hadn't wanted to love again, anyway. Loving meant heartache. He'd had his fill of heartache with Maggie. And this Rachel, or not-Rachel, was certain to leave as soon as she discovered who she really was or her forgotten family came searching for her.

"I'll give you some money to buy clothes tomorrow," Wade said gruffly. "You lost everything but what you were wearing when the train derailed."

She was smiling at Jordan's excitement, but when she turned, a hint of uncertainty undulated briefly across her face. "Thank you."

Jordan began naming the stores she should visit, and Ursula returned with the food. Jordan dug into his dessert with gusto. Wade, realizing with a jolt of surprise his own appetite had returned, cut into his steak. Rachel, her feet propped on the bench, hugged her knees and studied the stars visible through the pine boughs while he finished his meal.

This contentment and harmony were what he'd longed for, what had been missing since long before Maggie's death. He'd hoped Rachel's presence would restore it, and it had.

Except Rachel wasn't Rachel, and neither he nor Jordan should become accustomed or attached to her. Inevitably, she would leave them lonely and discontented, just as Maggie had.

"We're going into Libby tomorrow, Ursula," Rachel announced when the housekeeper brought Wade's dessert, "all three of us."

"Jordan, too?" The old woman's jaw dropped. When she clamped it shut, tears clouded her eyes. "Saints be praised," she muttered, and returned to the kitchen.

Wade set down his fork. Ursula had better keep praying. He would need all the help he could get.

RACHEL WAITED by the pickup in front of the house, enjoying the first morning since her accident without accompanying aches and pains.

Avoiding her gaze, Wade approached. "You ready to go?"

His chilly tone doused her like ice water, and she frowned. If Wade was looking forward to their outing, he kept his anticipation well hidden. She scanned his face, whose rugged planes and angles she was beginning to know by heart, hoping for some sign of what was bothering him. He'd been acting moody and distant ever since the claims adjuster's visit last night.

"Ready as I'll ever be," she answered.

"Where's Jordan?"

She shaded her eyes and gazed through the dappled morning sunlight toward the barn. "Saying goodbye to his pony."

"We're only going to Libby, not around the world. I'll fetch him." He sauntered toward the barn, his tooled boots kicking up dust in the road and clouds in her heart.

Last night he had done as she'd asked and made time for Jordan in his schedule. She should have been happy, but she wasn't, because at the same time, he had shut her out, erecting an invisible barricade around himself as solid as bricks and mortar.

She crammed her hands in her pockets and scuffed her sneaker in the dirt, forming mindless circles that matched her spinning thoughts. Wade's behavior shouldn't surprise her. From the first, he'd stressed that he wasn't interested in emotional involvement. All he wanted was a mother for his kid. But when he'd changed his approach with Jordan, she'd hoped he might warm to her as well. Instead, while his manner remained polite, its temperature had cooled.

When Wade had walked into the kitchen earlier this morning, he'd all but ignored Jordan and greeted her with a nod so reserved and rigid, she'd wondered if she'd unknowingly offended him.

Or maybe she had imagined his rebuff. The unsettling dream that had jerked her awake in a sweat at dawn had muddled her senses until she couldn't think straight. Fleeting memories of a man who had called her Jennifer still haunted her. Reminding herself that dreams weren't supposed to make sense hadn't eased her anxiety.

She jumped like a high-strung cat when a small hand grasped hers. Beside her, Jordan hopped from one foot to the other in anticipation. ''All set, Rachel?''

''You bet.'' The boy's brilliant smile banished memories of her disturbing dream. She knelt in the dust by the truck to meet him eye-to-eye. ''And I'm counting on you.''

''Me?'' His chest swelled with pride. ''What for?''

She leaned closer with a conspiratorial whisper. "I'm a total greenhorn. You'll have to help me find my way around town and introduce me to people."

He lowered his eyebrows in a worried frown. "There's lots I don't know, either."

"Just ask your dad. He'll tell you. Then you can teach me."

"Yeah." Jordan's grin widened and he threw his arms around her neck in a hug. "This is gonna be fun."

She returned his spontaneous gesture with a quick, fierce pressure before he broke away and ran toward the house.

"I forgot my allowance money," he called over his shoulder.

She pushed to her feet and swiveled toward the truck, only to run smack into Wade, who had come up behind her.

At the contact, she jerked away, but his arms closed instinctively, drawing her tight against the soft denim of his shirtfront, filling her nostrils with his distinctive, provocative scent. His hands circled her waist, lifting her against him.

His thighs, hard and sinewy beneath jeans that fit like a second skin, molded against her legs. Although the unintentional embrace lasted only seconds, time moved with slow, sparkling clarity. When he dropped his arms and pulled away, she felt bereft.

His glance met hers briefly, and although she couldn't be certain, she thought she glimpsed her own need reflected in his eyes. At his unhurried, self-deprecating smile, desire cascaded through her with shuddering intensity, weakening her knees and sucking the air from her lungs. Attraction arced between them like heat lightning between clouds. She hadn't imagined it. He had to have felt it, too.

Whatever his reaction, Wade obviously intended to ignore it. He circled the truck and climbed behind the wheel. "Let's go."

He started the engine as Jordan burst from the house. Rachel opened the passenger door, the boy scampered in beside his father and she followed.

"Libby, here we come." Wade put the truck in gear and took off down the tree-lined drive toward the highway.

Constrained by his seat belt, Jordan still managed to bounce on the seat, radiating happiness with every bump.

In the intimacy of the cab, with a catchy country-and-western song on the radio, Rachel leaned back and closed her eyes, pretending they were a real family. With time, maybe they could be. She glanced over Jordan's unruly hair at Wade. Something intangible hovered in the air between her and the boy's handsome father, an inclination, born not only of desire but of kindred spirits. From the first time she'd seen Wade, she'd felt drawn in some inexplicable manner, as if she'd been waiting for him all her life.

She tapped her foot to the snappy tune, pleased by prospects and possibilities. She had time and proximity on her side. Sooner or later Wade had to feel the same pull and acknowledge it.

Without warning, Wade slammed on the brakes. Jordan yelped with surprise, and the sudden stop threw her forward against her seat belt. Lost in thought, she'd paid no attention to the road ahead, where a swirling cloud of dust partially concealed a vehicle in front of the truck.

Wade swore softly under his breath.

"Bummer," Jordan groaned beside her, and slid as low as his safety restraint allowed.

The dirt settled to reveal the sleek lines of a bright red pickup. Its door swung open, and a tall, slender young woman with a mane of thick, black, wind-tossed hair stepped out and ambled toward them with swaying hips.

The flawlessness of her makeup, the high polish of her cordovan boots, the impeccable cut of her jeans and the obvious quality of her fringed leather jacket over her red silk shirt made Rachel feel like a bag lady in her grubby sneakers and well-worn clothes.

The woman ignored Wade and Jordan and headed straight for Rachel's side of the truck.

Rachel rolled down her window and gazed into eyes that glittered like pale blue ice.

"I'm Sue Ann Swenson, Wade's neighbor." The woman thrust her well-manicured hand with its jungle-red nail polish through the window. "You must be the new baby-sitter the whole county's buzzing about."

Chapter Six

Sue Ann's handshake was limp and cold, as frosty as her voice and the glint in her eyes.

Rachel glanced at Wade, waiting for him to correct the baby-sitter label, but he stared silently through the windshield and gripped the wheel until his knuckles whitened. His attractive neighbor's arrival had obviously agitated him, but he gave no hint why.

"I'm Rachel O'Riley." Rachel withdrew her hand quickly and smiled at the woman with more confidence than she felt.

Rachel wondered why Wade didn't explain her status as wife-to-be to his neighbor. Had he changed his mind about their marriage? The prospect, even though their arrangement had been purely business, flooded her with unexpected sadness. More likely, she reminded herself, he was honoring his promise not to talk about their marriage until she was ready.

She glanced back at Wade, who sat silent, fuming like an awakening volcano and ignoring them both.

"Hi, Jordan. Hello, Wade." Sue Ann finally acknowledged the truck's other occupants.

"G'morning, Sue Ann." Wade's even tone gave no clue to his feelings. He nodded toward her pickup. "You're raising sand a little early this morning."

"You should know," Sue Ann said with a laugh heavy with innuendo. "You're the expert on sand-raising in these parts."

Wade poked Jordan lightly with his elbow, and the boy piped up with a polite but unenthusiastic, "Hello, Miss Swenson."

"Ursula's up at the house," Wade said.

"I didn't come to see Ursula, Wade. I came to see you."

Wade heaved a sigh. "What for?"

"To invite you to the barn dance at our place Saturday night."

This time, Wade faced Sue Ann, and his stoic look grew almost friendly. "That's mighty neighborly. Rachel and I will be happy to come."

At his mention of Rachel, surprise, shadowed by something darker, flashed across Sue Ann's artfully made up face. "Supper's at six o'clock, the dance at eight. And Wade—" she pressed closer to Rachel, practically nose-to-nose, her smile a challenge "—remember to save some dances for me."

Sue Ann stepped back from the cab, and Wade pressed on the gas, expertly avoiding her vehicle as his truck sped down the drive.

Jordan breathed a sigh of relief and sat up straighter. "At least this time, she couldn't reach me to pinch my cheek and call me 'son.'"

"Jordan, that's enough," Wade said. "You show respect for your elders."

"Yes, sir." The boy slumped again.

Flustered by the undercurrents that had flowed between Wade and his neighbor, Rachel held her tongue. Sue Ann obviously had her sights set on her handsome neighbor, but Wade had seemed more irritated than interested. Or maybe he hadn't wanted Sue Ann to see him with Rachel? But that didn't make sense. After all, Wade intended to marry her.

Or did he?

Trying to read his puzzling behavior was giving her a headache. If Wade *had* decided against marrying her, he'd have ample opportunity to tell her when they returned from Libby and Jordan was out of earshot. Until then, she'd try not to worry about how such a decision would affect her.

Jordan's sudden question forced the issue. "Dad, is Rachel really my baby-sitter?"

Rachel tensed, waiting for Wade's answer.

A tiny muscle twitched at the base of Wade's jaw, and he kept his eyes on the highway they'd just turned onto. "Rachel was in a train wreck, son. The accident made her lose her memory, and she's staying with us until she's better."

And after that? she longed to ask, but feared his answer.

"Wow." Jordan turned to her with awe-filled eyes. "You can't remember anything?"

"Only the important things, like how to brush my teeth and tie my shoes," she said with a lightness she didn't feel.

"What about your family?" the boy asked. "Don't you remember your mom and dad?"

She glanced at Wade, who had stiffened to alertness at Jordan's question. With his Stetson pulled low over his forehead, topping his rugged profile as he watched the road, he resurrected that warm, snuggly feeling beneath her breastbone. She longed to run her finger across his brows, down the strong, clean line of his nose, and linger on the fullness of his lips. Desire spun through her blood like whirling gypsies, flushing her skin and tightening her abdomen.

Wade's good looks triggered her longing, but the quality of his character fired her interest, and she silently inventoried his virtues. At the hospital, he had stayed by her bedside, comforting her when she knew no one else. His capacity for love for his son was indisputable, even if he hadn't quite figured out how to relate to Jordan.

He'd offered her a home when she had nowhere else to go. Last night after supper, when he'd thanked his neighbors for fighting the fire, they had responded with stories of Wade's generosity and assistance, which they were happy to repay. All had exhibited respect and affection for him.

Who wouldn't be captivated by such a treasure of a man?

As if pulled by her thoughts, his gaze flicked toward her. The intensity in his dark eyes rattled her.

"Well?" He spoke with a strange hesitation, as if asking something he didn't want to know. "Do you remember your folks?"

"I don't remember anyone. I wouldn't know my own name," she explained to Jordan, "if your daddy hadn't told me."

"How did you know it, Daddy?"

Rachel held her breath. Jordan's question offered Wade a perfect chance to announce their marriage agreement.

"I saw it in her wallet," Wade said.

His answer apparently satisfied Jordan, but left her unsettled and out of sorts.

Suddenly Jordan's small hand crept into hers. "Don't worry, Rachel. Maybe your daddy will come looking for you."

Her eyes smarted with tears at the boy's kindness, but before she could thank him for his concern, her bothersome dream loomed in her mind, and images of the unidentified man who'd called her Jennifer crystallized with too much clarity for a mere dream.

She was remembering.

The man's identity remained a mystery, but her reaction, right down to the sweating palms she dried on her jeans, suggested that she'd loved him.

Jordan squeezed her hand. "If your daddy doesn't come, you can stay with us. *You'll* take care of her, won't you, Dad?"

Wade glanced at her long enough for her to note the golden flecks smoldering in his brown eyes before he returned his attention to the road.

"I—" he began.

"I'm an adult, Jordan." Afraid of Wade's answer, she had cut him off. "I can take care of myself."

Wade raised one eyebrow, and his eyes sparked with sudden mischief. "I'll remind you of that if you find a spider in your room or run into a grizzly on the porch."

Her fears lessened at Wade's teasing, and her

mood brightened. "Are you telling me chivalry is dead?"

"Not dead, ma'am," he drawled in a voice she recognized as an imitation of Leo's, "but feeling poorly."

"Is Shil Ree going to die?" Jordan asked, with such seriousness that Rachel stifled a laugh.

"Chivalry," Wade explained, "is acting polite and considerate toward others."

"Like your father was to me," Rachel added, "when he invited me to your ranch because I don't know where my home is."

Jordan tilted his chin and considered her with a sorrowful gaze. "Are you lost, Rachel?"

The question floored her. In a single word, Jordan had captured the sum total of her amnesia.

"Hey, what kind of shopping trip is this?" Wade asked before she could respond. "You two have faces as long as Emmaline."

Jordan giggled.

"Who's Emmaline?" Rachel was glad to shove aside the coldness Jordan's question had caused.

Jordan giggled again. "Daddy's old cow. And I mean *really* old."

Rachel glanced at Wade in surprise. "You *name* your cattle?"

"Not all of them," he said a bit too casually. "But I helped deliver Emmaline. Raised her from a calf."

"She's a pet?"

"Not really." From the affection in his voice, she guessed otherwise. "I just never could send her to the slaughterhouse."

Rachel smiled with satisfaction. For all his rugged looks and man-of-steel muscles, Wade Garrett had a marshmallow core, sweet and soft. The notion pleased her, renewing her hope. Maybe he wouldn't have the heart to break their agreement and send her away.

From what little her dream had revealed of her former life, returning to it wasn't an option, even if her full memory came back. Every day strengthened her inclination to remain with Wade. And if he let her stay, she'd bust her bones to make him and Jordan happy.

Or die trying.

WITH A SAD HEART, Wade watched Rachel and Jordan laughing together. How unlucky could he be? He'd found the perfect mother for his unhappy son, only to discover she wasn't the woman who'd agreed to his marriage bargain.

That puzzle had kept him awake most of the night, tossing and turning until his sheets were knotted. In the predawn darkness, he'd placed a call to Dr. Sinclair at the hospital before she began her morning rounds, and explained about Crutchfield's visit and Rachel's unknown identity.

"Should I tell her we don't know who she is?"

The doctor had been firm. "Absolutely not. The poor girl's suffered enough. You'll either have to find out her true identity or wait till she remembers. Throwing another curve at her now could set her recovery back, maybe permanently impair her remembering."

He'd fixed a pot of coffee, not in the newfangled

coffeemaker Ursula used, but the way his daddy had always made it, boiled on the stove in an old enameled coffeepot with a raw egg, shell and all, stirred in to settle the grounds. While the coffee boiled, he'd dispatched Lefty to the main gate with orders to keep Larry Crutchfield and his blue Mercedes off the ranch. Then he'd drunk almost the whole pot waiting for Dan Howard to report to work at the sheriff's office.

When Wade finally reached his old friend on the phone, he'd told Dan the whole story, and they'd set up a plan for the morning. Now all he had to worry about was getting Rachel into the sheriff's office without giving away his hand.

"Is something wrong?" Rachel's musical voice broke into his musings, and he turned to find her staring at him, green eyes wide, forehead creased with worry.

"Wrong?" He had trouble concentrating on her words when she looked at him like that.

"You're scowling at the road like it's your worst enemy."

"Don't worry, Rachel," Jordan piped. "Dad always looks like that."

Wade glanced at his son in alarm. Was that really the way Jordan saw him? He rolled his shoulders to relax them and forced a smile. "Only when I don't get enough sleep at night."

From the corner of his eye, he saw Jordan's expression fall. "Were you worrying about your burned timber? I'm sorry—"

"Nope." With a playful yank, he jerked Jordan's hat down over his eyes. "I was thinking about what we'd do for excitement in town this morning, short stuff.''

Jordan shoved back his hat and smiled. "For excitement?''

"Yeah, for fun." Wade warmed to his deception. "Now, Rachel here, we don't need to worry about her having fun.''

"Well, thanks a lot." She pretended to protest, joining in the lightness of the moment.

"It's true," Wade insisted. "Give a pretty woman a credit card, turn her loose in a store and she's happy as a pig in mud.''

"You have a point," Rachel agreed. "But what will Jordan do for fun?''

"That," Wade said with a wink, "is a surprise.''

Jordan's face lit up like Fourth of July fireworks. "A surprise? For me, Dad?''

Wade nodded and swallowed an unexpected lump in his throat. The sight of Jordan's excitement almost wiped the smile from Wade's face. Hell, was there so little pleasure in the boy's life that a simple trip into town could cause such elation?

Guilt coursed through him. He hadn't planned his scheme for Jordan's amusement but as a ruse to get Rachel into the sheriff's office.

That the boy needed someone to mother him was more evident now than ever—ironically, since as of last night, his prime candidate for that job had been placed on the ineligible list.

"I'll only use your credit card on one condition," Rachel said.

"What?" Wade silently cursed himself. If he

didn't stop woolgathering, Rachel would guess something was up. "What condition?"

"That you allow me to pay you back as soon as I'm able."

"That won't be necessary—"

"No bargain, no shopping."

From the look on Rachel's face, Wade decided arguing was futile. "Suit yourself."

Jordan giggled beside him.

"What's so funny?"

"You made a joke, Dad."

Rachel laughed, too, an alluring sound like water bubbling over rocks. "Shopping for clothes. Suit yourself. Get it?"

Wade grinned. Jordan laughed harder, and soon they were all laughing. With a start, Wade realized he couldn't remember the last time he'd laughed like this. Or the last time Jordan had laughed at all. Damn. Rachel was good for both of them, and if his plan for the morning worked, he'd be hurrying her out of his life.

Before Jordan became any more attached to her.

Before he followed his son's lead.

With Rachel and Jordan singing along with "Mammas Don't Let Your Babies Grow Up to Be Cowboys" on the radio, Wade turned off the highway onto Libby's main drag. The street was clogged with shoppers, mostly tourists who flocked to the lake outside town to escape the summer heat. On alert for a blue Mercedes, he eyed the parked cars, but Crutchfield's vehicle was nowhere in sight. Wade pulled the truck into an empty parking space in front of the department store.

He tugged his wallet from his jeans, removed his credit card and handed it to Rachel. "Jordan and I will meet you here in—"

"Aw, Dad, can't we go with her?"

With raised eyebrows, Wade looked at his son. "You want to shop for ladies' clothes?"

"For Sue Ann Swenson's barn dance," the boy said. "We can help Rachel pick out something special. She'll be the prettiest lady there."

Jordan had that right. Rachel would be the prettiest woman there, even if she went wearing a flour sack. But the idea of helping her select a dress created too much intimacy for a man who was working hard to keep his distance.

"I don't know, son. Buying clothes is women's work—"

"Phooey," Rachel said with a smile. "I'll be spending your money, and if Jordan is going to be my date—" she pulled off the boy's hat and ruffled his hair, causing him to blush with pleasure "—I might as well have you two approve my choices."

Wade couldn't think straight when she looked at him with her head cocked to one side, blond hair blowing in the breeze and a soft smile on lips that begged for kissing.

"Why not?" He forced a grin and followed Rachel and Jordan into the store, feeling as if he had lead in his boots and every soul in Jackson County was watching his back and guffawing at his predicament. At one time, Maggie'd had him wrapped around her little finger, leading him around by the nose, with him so lovestruck he hadn't seen what was coming.

But even memories of Maggie did little to cool his blood when Rachel stepped out of the dressing room. The green gingham dress with its fitted bodice and spaghetti straps matched her eyes. Her waist appeared so tiny he could span it with his two hands, and the full skirt over white, ruffled petticoats flounced above legs so perfect they made his mouth water.

"Awesome," Jordan breathed in approval, then he bunched his face in a frown. "But won't you get cold?"

Cold was the last thing on Wade's mind. The sight of those perfect shoulders, lightly tanned skin as smooth as fine china, and the tiniest hint of cleavage had his blood simmering.

"There's a matching sweater." Mrs. Grant, the saleswoman, flicked the sweater from beneath a counter and spread it out for Wade's approval. "Green cashmere with gingham trim."

Rachel twirled gracefully in front of the three-way mirror and turned to face him. "What do you think? Mrs. Grant says it's perfect for a barn dance."

Wade sucked in a deep breath and tried to act nonchalant. As far as he was concerned, she could wear the dress to the White House and she'd knock 'em all dead. "Mrs. Grant's the expert. We'll have to take her word."

A hint of disappointment glittered briefly in Rachel's eyes, and Wade could have kicked himself for a fool. He'd avoided women so long, he'd forgotten his manners. He started to issue a belated compliment, but Rachel had already returned to the dressing room.

Less than thirty minutes later, they exited the department store and heaped packages in the pickup. Some women, Wade knew, would have dawdled all day picking out a wardrobe, but Rachel, with practical good sense, had quickly selected jeans, shirts, a jacket, boots, shoes to match her dress, underwear and two flannel nightgowns. Not exactly a trousseau, but, he reminded himself, she wasn't going to be needing one. Rachel, or not-Rachel, might already be married to somebody else. The sooner he and Dan Howard found out, the better.

"Now, Jordan, it's time for your surprise. Follow me," he stated.

Fairly jumping with excitement, Jordan fell in step beside him, with Rachel on the boy's other side. They walked the two blocks to the sheriff's office, pausing to nod and speak briefly to neighbors. Wade noted the speculation in his friends' eyes as they spoke to Rachel, and he wished he could have introduced her as his fiancée, according to his original plan. He'd seen her questioning glance each time he omitted that information, but he'd save them both embarrassment later by a little awkwardness now.

Between greetings, he kept a wary eye out for any sign of Crutchfield.

"Here we are." He stopped in front of the sheriff's office, where two patrol cars were parked at the curb.

"What are we doing here?" Jordan asked.

"Come on in. You'll see." Wade held open the glass door, then followed Rachel and Jordan inside.

Wade stopped at the desk of the dispatcher and asked her to tell the sheriff they'd arrived. Within seconds, Dan Howard, moving with the dynamism of a tornado, swept into the entry room. Although he saw Dan often, Wade was always taken aback by how little his high school buddy had changed over the years. His hair was shorter, closely-cropped to department standards, but not a gray hair marred his crew cut, and his brilliant blue eyes and boyish grin made the tall, well-built sheriff look like a mature teenager.

"Dan, this is Rachel O'Riley," Wade said. "And you know Jordan."

Dan shook Rachel's hand, and if Wade hadn't known him so well, he would have missed the flash of approval as Dan greeted her. The sheriff turned to Jordan with the same welcoming smile. "I remember Jordan as just a little feller. You've grown six inches since I saw you last."

Jordan gazed up at the uniformed sheriff in awe. "Dad said we're here for a surprise."

"You betcha," Dan said. "I promised your father I'd show you how we process criminals when we arrest them."

Jordan's face crumpled and his lower lip trembled. "You're going to arrest me, aren't you?"

Dan blinked in surprise. "Why would I arrest you?"

Jordan swallowed a sob. "'Cause I burned down my dad's timber. That makes me a crin-crinimal."

Dumbfounded by his son's reaction, Wade stood speechless. He glanced away from Jordan to find Rachel glaring at him with accusing eyes.

"How could you?" she reproached him.

"But I didn't—"

Dan came quickly to his aid. "Horse puckey, son. You're no criminal. Your daddy's prouder of you than a grizzly with a fresh-caught salmon."

Jordan stood straighter. "He is?"

"Sure he is. He asked me to show you around, thought maybe I could make you a junior deputy."

Wade breathed a sigh of relief when Rachel lost her disapproving scowl and Jordan straightened his shoulders. The boy grinned at Dan. "Can I wear a badge?"

"You betcha. Now you folks follow me, and I'll show you how we book a prisoner. Ready, Junior Deputy Garrett?"

"Yes, sir!"

Jordan followed Dan through a door into a hallway that led to the back of the building. Wade motioned Rachel to go ahead of him, but she hung back.

"I'm sorry," she said. "I jumped to conclusions."

Wade raked his fingers through his hair, remembering Jordan's tortured face a few minutes earlier. "It's my own damn fault. I should have realized what he'd think."

Rachel nodded. "He's a complicated little boy. Takes a lot of blame on himself, even for things that aren't his fault."

"Like what?"

Jordan called from the hallway. "C'mon. We're going to have our mug shots taken."

The excitement in his voice made Rachel smile, and the sweetness of her expression had Wade's heart doing flip-flops. He had to pull himself together before he grabbed her and kissed her right in front of Annie, the sheriff's dispatcher, who'd broadcast the news in minutes, and by sundown, the whole durned county would know.

Besides, Wade couldn't afford to show his feelings. Rachel didn't know their marriage was off or that she might be leaving them soon. Somehow he had to keep their lives on an even keel until the sheriff tracked down her identity.

"Wade?"

He looked up to see her waiting for him in the hallway, her head cocked with that adorably quizzical look that played havoc with his hormones. "Coming."

He started down the hall behind her, hoping that whatever Dan Howard did to find out who she was, he'd do it fast.

AN HOUR LATER, Rachel sat in a booth across from Wade and Jordan and gazed in disbelief at the hamburger on the plate before her.

"That's one serving?" she asked.

Wade nodded. "Montana size. We appreciate good beef."

"But that's enough food to feed a small town."

"Maybe a small *Eastern* town," he said with a deprecating grin.

Jordan had attacked his own megaburger and was shoveling in french fries as if he hadn't eaten in a week. Pinned to his shirt pocket was a shiny silver badge that said Junior Deputy.

Rachel reached for her burger and noticed a smudge of ink on her left index finger. "I've washed my hands twice since the fingerprinting, and I'm still covered in ink.''

Jordan washed down his food with a swallow of milk. ''The fingerprinting was cool, but I wish I had my own handcuffs.''

''Maybe when you're a few years older and can ride with the junior posse,'' Wade suggested. His eyes met Rachel's, and the warmth of his smile lit a bonfire in her abdomen.

''I have to be sixteen.'' Jordan looked crushed. ''That's eight more years.''

''There must be something else exciting you can do in the meantime,'' Rachel said. ''What about that camping award you're working on?''

She'd learned all about his project the night of the fire, but she wanted Wade to hear. He scowled at the memory of the fire, but when she shook her head in warning, he relaxed and picked up her cue.

''Right, Jordan,'' he said. ''Tell me about it.''

Jordan paused with a french fry halfway to his lips. ''It's a badge for Scouts. I have to sleep outside, fix my own meals...'' He hesitated and lowered his eyes. ''Build my own fires. Stuff like that.''

Wade nodded. ''I'm sure between Rachel and Ursula, they can let you sleep out in the backyard—''

''Wade Garrett!'' Rachel felt her temperature rising. ''All this gorgeous countryside everywhere you look, and you'd make your own son camp out in his *backyard?*''

Jordan looked disappointed, an expression all too common for the youngster. She noted Wade had the decency to look uncomfortable, and she took satisfaction in his squirming.

"I suppose," he said, scratching his chin, "we could come up with a suitable spot, but he can't go alone."

Rachel fixed him with a stare that she hoped would drill stone. "No, he can't."

Jordan's face shone with hope. "How about Keeler Mountain Lookout, Dad? Could we camp there? Can Rachel come with us?"

"Whoa, buster." Wade shook his head. "I've got a ranch to run. It'll be weeks before—"

Rachel got a grip on her temper and smiled her sweetest smile. Jordan needed an ally. He'd been at the mercy of his handsome father's indifference for too long. "But, Wade, I'm sure Leo can handle things for a couple more days. And I'd like to see more of the country if I'm going to make my home here."

"Gosh, can we, Dad? Can we go tomorrow?"

Rachel swallowed a tiny bite of her burger and wiped her lips. "Tomorrow would be good, wouldn't it? That would have us back in time for Sue Ann Swenson's barn dance."

WADE PAID THE BILL and followed Rachel and Jordan to the pickup. His head was swimming and his food sat uneasy in his churning stomach. He'd been bamboozled by the best of them. How could he say no when Rachel looked at him with those exotic green eyes? She had him so hornswoggled he didn't know up from down.

He wanted to find out who she really was. And he didn't. Because once he knew her identity, she might have to go back where she came from.

He wanted her to go. And he didn't. He feared the consequences of falling in love again. He hadn't fared well with Maggie. But he didn't like the thought of going through life without Rachel, either.

But she's not Rachel, you dimwit. She's probably someone else's wife. A woman that special wouldn't stay unattached for long. Someone with sense—and luck—would snap her up.

He wanted to spend more time with Jordan. And he didn't. He could hear his own father's voice, praising the virtues of hard work, discipline and the straight and narrow. Affection and good times had had no place in Fulton Garrett's philosophy. Had Wade's own face ever shown the fear and unhappiness Jordan's had? And if it had, had Fulton Garrett even noticed?

Hell, Wade even wanted to be married again. And he didn't. Marriage to Maggie had brought its own special hell, an agony he never wanted to experience again. But marriage to Rachel? The thought tantalized, seduced him. But what guarantee did he have that Rachel—if she wasn't already married— wouldn't be as disastrous a wife as Maggie?

"Wade?" Rachel gazed at him from the cab. "Are you all right?"

He jerked out of his thoughts to find himself standing by the driver's door, his hand on the handle. Jordan and Rachel both watched him, their eyes filled with concern.

"Indigestion," he said with a grimace. "I'll take some bicarbonate when we get back to the ranch."

He slid into the driver's seat, started the truck and pulled out on the highway. He needed something, all right. But it sure as hell wasn't bicarb. To cure what ailed him would take something a heck of a lot stronger than soda.

He offered up a silent prayer that Dan would find Rachel's real name quickly, and stepped on the gas.

Chapter Seven

Wade slowed his truck for the turn onto the ranch. Lefty Starr, Winchester rifle cradled in his arm, touched the brim of his hat in salute as the pickup passed.

"Why's Lefty at the gate with a gun?" Jordan asked.

The wheels in Wade's mind backpedaled as he thought fast. "Keeping out pesky real estate agents."

"You've never run 'em off like that before." Puzzlement filled the boy's voice.

"Time they learned *no* means *no.*" Wade shifted uneasily in his seat. Lies didn't sit easy on his lips. Unlike the way they had with Maggie. Lying had been her specialty.

On the other side of Jordan, Rachel sat silent, but Wade could feel her gaze, which increased his uneasiness. The drive to the house seemed the longest he'd ever made, and when they arrived, he had to stop himself from leaping from the truck in relief.

"Can I play with my new video game now?"

Jordan held up the bag with his purchase from his allowance.

Wade nodded. "Long as you take time to pack. We'll leave for Keeler after breakfast tomorrow."

"Yippee!" Bounding out of the cab, Jordan all but ran over Rachel in his excitement.

Rachel began gathering her packages from the passenger seat in the back of the cab, and Wade slowed his escape long enough to help.

"If I ever knew anything about camping," she said with an apologetic smile, "I don't remember."

Wade tucked the last of her purchases under his arm. "Ursula will tell you what to take."

She stopped him with a hand on his arm as he headed up the front steps. "Wade?"

He stifled a groan. When she turned that gut-kicking smile on him, his legs were weaker than a day-old calf's. He hardened his expression. "Yeah?"

"Thanks for agreeing to go camping. It means a lot to Jordan."

"No problem." He dumped the bags and boxes onto a rocker on the porch and headed to the barn as fast as his boots would carry him, prodded every step by the tines of a guilty conscience. He hadn't agreed to the trip just for his son's sake. He was simply a sucker for a pretty woman. A pretty woman he wanted to keep away from Larry Crutchfield, even if it meant climbing a damn mountain and spending the night away when he had work to do at home.

RACHEL WATCHED WADE GO, then picked up the bundles he'd discarded, and entered the house. She climbed the wide central staircase with its rustic bark banister and carried her purchases into the guest room. Painted the color of rich cream, with gabled windows hung with ruffled curtains sprigged with tiny blue flowers, the room exuded cheerfulness. A ruffled bedspread matched the curtains, and vases held generous cuttings of the climbing roses that rambled over the front of the house. Ursula had obviously decorated the room to make her feel welcome.

As Rachel unpacked her new clothes, placed some in bureau drawers scented with floral sachets and hung others in the cedar-lined closet, a strange contentment came over her. In spite of her lack of memory, she felt comfortably at home in Wade's house. She must have known what she'd been doing when she'd answered his ad for a wife. She had a feeling she was going to be very happy at Longhorn Ranch.

Putting away the last of her clothes, she sprinted down the stairs. She found Ursula chopping weeds with a hoe in a large garden plot, the one area of the backyard not densely shaded by tall lodgepole pines. At Rachel's approach, the old woman rubbed her back with the flat of one hand and pushed a calico sunbonnet off her brow with the other.

"Find what you needed in Libby?" she asked.

Rachel nodded. "And Wade's agreed to take Jordan camping tomorrow. I'll need you to tell me what to pack."

Ursula's weathered face broke into a grin. "I'll be happy to. I've had about all the weeding I can take for one day, anyhow."

They climbed the steps to the back porch, and Ursula brought a frosty pitcher of lemonade and tall glasses from the kitchen. When they'd both settled into chairs, Ursula indicated the mountain range that rose west of the ranch and pointed to a large dome-shaped mountain off to the right.

"That's Keeler. Wade's daddy used to take him camping there when he was younger than Jordan."

"You knew Wade's parents?"

"Just Fulton, his daddy. His poor momma didn't live long enough after Wade was born for me to know her. Fulton raised him on his own."

"What was Fulton like?"

"You've seen his portrait, over the fireplace in the living room?"

Rachel nodded. From his picture, Fulton Garrett had struck her as a restrained, unapproachable man.

"Hard as nails and twice as cold, Fulton was." Ursula took a sip of lemonade. "Made Wade walk the straight and narrow from the time he could toddle. Didn't believe in spoiling a child with affection."

Rachel experienced a pang of sympathy for the little boy Wade had been. Knowing how Fulton had raised him went a long way toward explaining Wade's relationship with Jordan. Maybe Wade hadn't been so far off the mark with his crazy marriage scheme, after all. Jordan *did* need a mother, someone to love him, to take the rough edges off the way his daddy treated him.

"You helped raise Wade?" Rachel asked.

"Wiped his tears, sneaked him hugs when his

daddy wasn't looking. Fulton believed 'coddling' ruined a child.''

"Wade was lucky to have you."

"And Jordan's lucky to have you."

Ursula's words were warm, but a shadow flitted across her face, as if she had remembered something unpleasant.

"What about Jordan's mother?" Rachel asked. "What kind of woman was she?"

Ursula's face shut tight as a miser's wallet. "We don't talk about Maggie around here. Ever. It's like she never happened."

Rachel backed off the forbidden ground. "Have the Realtors been back today?"

"Realtors?" Ursula looked puzzled. "Haven't seen 'em."

Rachel remembered Jordan's surprise at finding Lefty guarding the ranch entrance and the feebleness of Wade's explanation, and wondered what Wade was trying to hide.

Ursula took another sip of lemonade. She must have swallowed wrong, because she choked, turning red and wheezing before she caught her breath again. "Wade heard they were in the neighborhood. Doesn't want 'em bothering him. Now about this camping trip."

Rachel suppressed a frown at the old woman's rapid change of subject. Whatever the real reason Lefty was guarding the gate, neither Wade nor Ursula wanted her to know it.

EARLY THE NEXT MORNING, the pickup ascended toward the crest of Keeler Mountain, and Wade, listening for sounds of descending logging trucks, slowed as he rounded each switchback.

At times, the road sliced through the deep shade of dense evergreens. At others, it skirted an open cliff face, presenting a panoramic view of Longhorn Valley, spread out far below, a crazy quilt of meadows, forests, lakes and rivers in a patchwork of greens and blues.

Rachel's exclamations of delight blended with Jordan's at each new vista, and Wade couldn't help comparing her childlike enthusiasm with Sue Ann's Swenson's indifference, bordering on contempt, toward the valley she'd lived in all her life. He quelled a shudder. Sue Ann would be waiting at the barn dance, anxious to get him in her clutches. She'd all but posted notice to the valley that she intended to be the next Mrs. Wade Garrett. And she wasn't going to take kindly to Rachel. He sighed and shifted his attention back to the view. He'd handle that problem later.

The more time he spent with Rachel, the more the irony of his predicament taunted him. She'd taken readily to Jordan, the ranch and Montana. He'd have to be dumb as a stump not to realize she'd taken to him, too. Under different circumstances, her easy adjustment would have had him hanging out the window, shouting his happiness to the world.

But not knowing who she was, he'd have been better off if she'd holed up in her room and refused to have anything to do with him or Jordan. He grimaced inwardly. Maybe *he* should have hidden out someplace until Rachel's true identity was resolved.

Too late now.

After the last switchback, the truck whined in low gear as it climbed the final approach to the mountaintop. Halfway to the peak, Wade stopped and tapped the horn several times. Its blare echoed across the valley.

Rachel looked around, puzzled. "Is someone up here?"

"That's for the honeymooners," Jordan said.

"Honeymooners?"

Wade pointed through a sparse stand of trees that stood between them and the mountain's flat, grassy peak. A five-story tower topped by a wooden cabin, its poles secured by guy wires, loomed in the distance. "That's Keeler Mountain Lookout."

"Does someone live there?" she asked.

Wade shook his head. "Not anymore. Between air patrols and satellite coverage, most of these old fire lookouts are no longer needed."

Rachel seemed bewildered. "But Jordan said you tooted for the honeymooners."

Wade set the parking brake and twisted to face her. "When I was about four and Dad brought me here to pick huckleberries, he stopped his truck where we are now and blew the horn. When I asked why, he said he was alerting the honeymooners."

Jordan bounced on the seat. "Tell her about them."

Amusement replaced the confusion in Rachel's green eyes, and her soft, rosy lips tilted in a beguiling smile. "Real honeymooners?"

Wade nodded and repressed Jordan's boisterousness with a firm hand on the child's shoulder.

"Folks were more inhibited in Dad's day. He didn't bother to explain what honeymooners were."

"I know." Jordan puffed out his chest with self-importance. "They're people on a vacation after they get married."

"That's right," Wade said, enjoying Rachel's amused reaction, "but I didn't know. All that registered in my four-year-old mind was *moon*. I thought my father was a magician who could summon creatures from the moon with his truck horn."

"But you learned otherwise when you met them," Rachel said.

"Nope. When I climbed those stairs—with Dad right behind, clutching my belt to make sure I didn't fall—to that enchanted cabin in the sky, a young woman with a halo of golden hair and beautiful laughing eyes met me at the door. She even smelled pretty."

"Like flowers, you said," Jordan added.

"Out of this world was the only way to describe her," Wade said, "and at four, I fell in love for the first time in my life."

"I suppose she had a husband," Rachel said wryly, "since she was on her honeymoon?"

The late morning sun, streaming through the window behind Rachel, formed a shining aureole, back-lighting her with an unearthly radiance. Like a thunderbolt, the resemblance between Rachel and the honeymooner of his childhood struck him. No wonder he'd been drawn to Rachel, even before she'd regained consciousness.

"I liked her husband, too." Wade dragged his attention from the vision beside Jordan and gazed toward the lookout tower. "He let me stand on a stool with glass insulators and locate our ranch through the firefinder."

"Glass insulators?" Rachel asked.

"The glass on the feet of the stool protected the lookout against lightning during thunderstorms."

Wade's voice was calm, but his insides quivered. Glass insulators wouldn't have deflected the jolt he'd just received. With forceful clarity, he recognized he could no more distance himself from Rachel than the earth could break orbit from the sun.

And even if he somehow managed, his world would be as bleak as empty space.

"Why do you still honk for honeymooners?" she asked.

"It's a..." Jordan knotted his forehead in concentration "...a tradition."

Wade released the parking brake and eased the truck forward. "The couple returned the following year, and Dad brought me to see them. That was their last summer in the forest. Even so, for years, every time we came to Keeler, I'd ask Dad to toot the horn, hoping they'd somehow, magically, return."

"I wish I'd known you when you were little." Rachel's wistful tone wrenched his heart. "Your childhood sounds wonderful. I can't recall anything about mine."

"You will," he assured her.

And when she did, she'd leave him, and he'd lose the best thing that had happened to him since Maggie. Before life with Maggie went sour.

He glanced at his son, who strained against his

seat belt, his thin face beaming with anticipation, and corrected his assessment. Rachel was the best thing since Jordan was born.

As the tower came into full view, with its four walls of windows glinting in the sun, he heard Rachel laugh. ''I see now why your father sounded an alarm. The lookouts lived in a glass house.''

''Can we climb the tower, Dad? We only came here once before, and you said I was too little then.''

''Maybe later.'' Remorse gnawed at him. Jordan was eight, going on nine, yet he'd brought his son only once to the place that had been his own favorite as a boy.

Rachel and her startling likeness to his honeymoon lady had revived memories, not only of the visits themselves, but also of the wonderment and exhilaration of his childhood. Jordan should have been experiencing those marvels and delights, but Wade had been too busy, wrapped in self-pity and the problems of the ranch, to know whether Jordan's development was including the kind of milestones and adventures that had made his own growing up special.

If it hadn't been for Rachel, Wade would never have remembered what being a child was like, and he would have failed his son in the worst way. He had a lot to make up for, but today would be a start.

RACHEL LAY BACK on the blanket, propped on her elbows, and gazed over the distant valley, struggling to stay awake. The early afternoon sun toasted her face and, in spite of a cooling breeze, produced a comfortable warmth, even at the high altitude. After a lunch of Ursula's thick ham sandwiches, home-made chocolate cookies and hot coffee, she would have dozed off if Jordan hadn't wakened her.

"Look at these, Rachel."

The boy stood beside her, glowing with happiness and curiosity and presenting a totally different picture from his tear-stained appearance when they'd first met. His father's attention was all Jordan had needed. Even his appetite had improved. If he kept eating the way he had at lunch, the gauntness in his face would disappear in no time.

"What did you find?" She sat up and patted the blanket beside her, astonished by the surge of maternal affection he triggered.

He knelt and held out dirt-grimed hands. On each palm lay a rock, one greenish-gray with sharp, jagged edges and the other rounded and smooth with rusty striations through its glassy surface. "Do you know what kind they are?"

Rachel turned over each stone and examined it. "They're beautiful, but I don't know anything about rocks."

Wade returned from placing the lunch cooler in the shade of the truck, and glanced over the boy's shoulder.

"How can I find out what they're called?" Jordan looked to his father.

"Next time I go into town," Wade said, "you can come with me. The library has plenty of books that identify all kinds of rocks."

"Wow, that would be great! I can start a collection." Jordan picked up a plastic bag that had held cookies and dropped the rocks into it. "Can I look for more?"

"What about picking huckleberries?" Wade asked.

"That's work," Jordan said with a grimace. "Hunting rocks is fun."

"Okay, but only if you stay within certain limits." Wade pointed out the boundaries for Jordan to observe while searching.

"If you need us, we'll be just west of the ridge-line."

Jordan looped the bag through his belt and sprinted off toward an outcropping of boulders on the south end of the mountaintop.

"What if he runs into those grizzlies you mentioned?" Rachel doubted she could feel more apprehensive about the boy's safety if he'd been her own son.

"Don't worry." Wade's eyes twinkled with humor as he handed her a galvanized bucket. "All the bears will be where we are, eating huckleberries."

"Oh." Suddenly berry picking seemed less appealing.

"I'm kidding." Wade grasped her hand and hauled her to her feet.

Too surprised to resist, she found herself gazing into his face, while diverse elements assaulted her senses. The firm pressure of his callused hand, a whiff of chocolate on his warm breath, the sun-baked heat of his skin and teasing laughter in his seductive eyes weakened her knees. She clasped his arm to keep from falling.

"There're no bears?" Breathless as a long-distance runner, she gasped the words.

His expression sobered, as if he'd mistaken her giddiness for fear. "Grizzlies are seldom seen this side of the valley. They stay in the Cabinet Mountains, in the wilderness area. I promise you'll be safe. And despite Jordan's disclaimer, picking huckleberries is more fun than work."

She backed away and whirled around, the empty pail spinning at her side as she took in the full-circle view. "In this air with this scenery, anything would be enjoyable."

"Anything?" The heat simmering in his eyes and the upturned corners of his mouth suggested infinite possibilities.

Apparently his earlier reservations had disappeared, and she wondered why. Although Wade's change of attitude pleased her, her body's instantaneous response to his teasing unnerved her.

To avoid his molten look, she glanced at Jordan, sitting at the base of some boulders, happily sorting rocks and pebbles, then pivoted on her heel and headed down the ridge toward the huckleberry patch Wade had indicated earlier.

"Last one to fill a bucket has to cook supper," she called over her shoulder.

The tremor of Wade's footsteps as he caught up with her transferred through the soles of her sneakers and vibrated up her legs. By the time they reached the broad swath of low bushes clinging to the steep mountainside, she felt a rush of anticipation.

Wasn't this what she'd wanted—for Wade to discover she was more than just a caretaker for his son? That she was flesh and blood, with wants and needs of her own?

Then why was she shaking like a virgin bride?

The stunning implications of her last question raised a dozen more, including the burning puzzle of whether she'd ever made love with a man before. She couldn't even remember being kissed. In that instant, she knew that more than anything she wanted Wade to kiss her.

She halted at the edge of the clump beside a shrub heavy with fruit. "What now?"

Wade moved down the slope and turned to face her, his eyes level with hers. "Have you ever tasted huckleberries?"

She blinked in confusion. Berries had nothing to do with her question.

Without removing his riveting gaze from her face, Wade reached out, plucked a berry and lifted it to her lips. She bit into the warm, sweet fruit, and its juice exploded in her mouth and dribbled down her chin.

Just as Wade lifted his hand to wipe the juice from her face, a flash of movement and golden fur in the distant trees made her flinch in alarm.

"A bear!" She started to turn back toward the mountaintop, but her foot slipped on the loose pebbles of the dry hillside.

As if in slow motion, she pitched forward, ramming into Wade and knocking him to his back. With her sprawled atop him, they slid down the almost-vertical slope, raising clouds of dust and creating a miniature rock cascade as they went.

Wade held her close, absorbing the impact of her fall, the jolts of the rough terrain. After what seemed forever, but was only seconds, he whipped out his hand and grabbed a nearby bush. His hold anchored them and yanked them to a stop.

"I'm sorry." She raised herself on her elbows. "But the bear—"

Wade released his grip on the branch and restrained her with firm hands. "That was no bear."

"But I saw…" Her body melded with his, each curve fitting as if they were two pieces of one jigsaw puzzle.

"You saw a white-tailed deer." He moved his hands up her back, caressed her neck and clasped her face between his palms. Laughter, and something hotter, blazed in his eyes as he pulled her face closer. "It's nothing to be scared of."

The wild animal that frightened her now was the one he had loosed inside her with his touch.

His lips joined hers, branding her soul. Unwilling to resist his slow, skillful enticement, she opened her mouth to him. The gentle but insistent flick of his tongue ousted all conscious thoughts but one.

For the rest of her life, the taste of huckleberries would remind her of Wade's kiss.

Suddenly, as if someone had turned him off with a switch, Wade jerked away. "I'm sorry. I shouldn't have done that."

With an abruptness that shocked her, he shifted her off him, rose to his feet and brushed dust from his jeans, all the while refusing to meet her gaze.

"Sorry?" she echoed, confused at his sudden mood change.

"Shouldn't have kissed you," he said, wiping his lips with the back of his hand as if removing the evidence. "Broke my own rule."

"What rule?" She pushed herself to her feet, shaken more by his kiss and subsequent rejection than the slide down the mountainside.

"Our arrangement. Strictly business, remember?"

"Sure." Her head swam, bedeviled by mixed signals. He'd *wanted* to kiss her. And he'd obviously enjoyed it. So what, all of a sudden, had made him change his mind?

"Our arrangement..." she began.

He cleared his throat, but his voice still came out husky. "Better not to talk about it now. We'll wait a few more days. See if your memory returns."

"Okay." She tried but couldn't keep the hurt from her voice, the disappointment from her face.

"Look," he said, his tone softening. "I don't want you making any long-term decisions under duress. Give yourself time, okay?"

She nodded. His suggestion was sensible, logical. But there'd been nothing logical or sensible about the kiss they'd shared. Maybe he was right. She needed to make her choices with a clear mind. With her memory intact.

If she kept responding with her senses instead of her head, he'd begin to wonder what kind of wanton woman had answered his ad in the first place.

She scrambled up the rock face and retrieved her bucket. "Ursula will skin us alive if we don't bring back enough berries for jelly."

Wade relaxed and grinned, evidently relieved that

a crisis had passed. "We'll be punishing ourselves if we don't include enough for a pie or two."

The rest of the afternoon passed in quiet companionship as they filled countless buckets with huckleberries and emptied them into a huge washtub in the bed of the pickup.

"We must have ten gallons of berries," Rachel observed. "Can Ursula use all these?"

"Huckleberry jelly, jam, syrup." Wade ticked the items off on his fingers. "Pancakes, muffins, pies—"

Rachel held up her hands in surrender. "I get the idea." She glanced around the meadow that covered the mountain's flat top. "Where's Jordan?"

They had checked on the boy each time they'd returned to the truck to empty their buckets, but this time, Jordan was out of sight. He'd wandered outside the boundaries Wade had set for him. Alarmed, Wade started down the side of the mountain, calling his son's name.

Rachel followed close behind, grabbing hold of branches and shrubs to keep from pitching forward down the steep slope. They'd traveled far enough down the side that they couldn't see the lookout behind them when they spotted Jordan, digging happily in a pile of rocks.

Suddenly Wade froze.

Rachel followed his gaze to the cause of his concern. A few hundred feet below Jordan, a huge brown bear and two cubs were stripping huckleberries from a bush. Jordan, oblivious to the bears' presence, was humming as he dug for rocks.

"Jordan." Wade's voice, tense with fear, rang across the hillside.

The female bear lifted her head from the bushes and sniffed the air.

Jordan looked up, saw his father and waved.

"Bears, son. Roll into a ball, facedown, and don't move."

Rachel had to admire Wade's control. While his voice held a firm, not-to-be-argued-with tone, the tension had left it. He obviously didn't want to spook Jordan into making a sudden move and inciting the mother bear to charge.

Jordan responded immediately to his father's orders, pulling himself into a ball with his arms over his head, his face pressed to the ground. Below him, the mother bear sniffed the air again, but the wind was coming up the mountain, blowing their scents away from her.

Rachel stood immobilized until her calves, braced awkwardly on the steep slope, ached from the strain. Terrified for Jordan, she had to remind herself to breathe. The deathly quiet of the mountainside was broken only by the rustle of huckleberry bushes and the rasping of Rachel's own breath. Beside her, Wade stood, paralyzed with fear for his son, but with a tension to his stance that indicated his readiness to run toward Jordan if the bear made a move.

And do what? Rachel wondered. His rifle was on the rack in the back of the pickup. What chance would even a big man like Wade have against a bear that looked twice his size?

For what seemed like hours, the bear and her cubs feasted in the berry patch. Wade and Rachel watched helplessly as Jordan lay as still as he could, his thin shoulders trembling with terror. They didn't dare move toward the boy for fear of spooking the bear. Finally, the bear, her cubs rolling and frolicking close behind, lumbered down the mountain and out of sight.

When Wade started moving down the slope, Rachel sank down with relief and rubbed the burning muscles in her legs. As she watched, Wade reached Jordan, scooped him in his arms and strode back up the mountain.

Jordan's face was etched with fear, and Rachel couldn't tell whether his fright was a remnant of his close encounter with the bear or reaction to the anger reddening his father's face. They reached Rachel, and Wade set Jordan on his feet.

"Was it a grizzly?" the boy asked shakily, his face pale.

Wade shook his head. "But big enough to do serious damage."

Jordan started to cry. "I'm sor-sorry."

Rachel started toward the boy, but Wade shook his head and raised his voice. "I *told* you not to wander off. Now do you understand why?"

Tears streaming down his cheeks, Jordan nodded. "Yes, sir. I'm sorry. I was looking at rocks and not paying attention."

Wade scowled at Jordan's tears. "Haven't I told you boys don't cry?"

Ignoring Wade's disapproval, Rachel pulled Jordan into her arms and held him close. "We know you're sorry," she crooned, and wiped his tears with the back of her hand. Speaking to Jordan, she glared over his head at his father. "And you've been punished enough by the scare that bear gave you. I'm sure from now on you'll obey your father's instructions more closely."

"Yes, ma'am." Jordan tightened his arms around her neck, and Rachel felt her own eyes flood with tears. He was so little and so frightened, and for most of his short life he hadn't had a mother to love him.

"Now," she ordered gently with a final swift hug before releasing him, "dry those tears. We have some exploring to do."

Jordan sniffed and wiped his face on his sleeve. "Ain't going nowhere there's bears."

With a twinkle in her eye, Rachel pointed up the mountain. "I doubt bears climb lookout towers."

"Can we?" Jordan, his fear overridden by excitement, pivoted toward Wade. "Can we climb the lookout, Dad?"

Wade looked from his son to Rachel and wondered at what exact point he'd lost control of the situation. In the tradition of his father, he'd been prepared to tan Jordan's hide for disobeying him and scaring them all half to death. Then Rachel had stepped in, and the opportunity for punishment had passed. But rewarding Jordan's misbehavior by a trip up the tower didn't seem right, and he opened his mouth to say so.

Then he caught the determined set of Rachel's pretty mouth, the mouth he'd kissed just hours ago. And the resolute glint in her eye. He noted Jordan's expression of delighted anticipation, as well. A cold, hard knot in Wade's stomach melted, and his father's disapproval, ringing in his memory, stilled.

He shut his mouth and jerked his head toward the mountaintop. "Better get a move on in case those bears come back for seconds."

"Whoopee!" Jordan scrambled up the steep slope ahead of them.

Rachel turned to Wade with a satisfied smile. "I'm getting the gist of this maternal stuff. It comes so naturally, you'd think I'd done it all before."

Wade forced a smile past suddenly stiff lips and followed her up the mountain. For all he knew, his not-Rachel had children—and a loving husband—of her own.

Chapter Eight

Rachel was winded by the time she completed the fifth flight of stairs and Wade pulled her through the deck opening to the catwalk. His grasp was firm and warm, and she could feel the power of his muscles as he lifted her onto the plank decking. If she hadn't been already gasping for air from the climb, Wade's proximity and the view from the lookout tower would have taken her breath away.

To the east, across the lush, green valley bisected by the sparkling blue of the river, rose the rugged splendor of the Cabinet Mountain Wilderness Area, the summits snow-covered even in late June.

Wade pointed to the highest peaks, directly opposite the tower. "That's A Peak. And Snowshoe."

To the north lay the tiny logging town of Troy, nestled like a miniature village on the banks of the Kootenai River. "Those mountains north of Troy," Wade explained, "are in British Columbia."

To the south, a gigantic chunk of rocks and earth blocked her view. Except for a narrow pass that the road snaked through, the landslide almost blocked the valley.

"Split Mountain," Wade said. "Hundreds of years ago, the mountain fell apart, and that lower section buried an Indian village. Even today, the place is considered taboo by the tribes."

To the west rose one range of mountains after another, undulating waves of green on an ocean of forest. Wade pointed to the nearest. "The closest peaks are in the Kootenai National Forest, but the next mountain range is in Idaho, in the Kaniksu National Forest."

Enchanted, Rachel grabbed the railing that circled the catwalk and drew in the sweet mountain air. "It's all so beautiful. And so big."

Wade nodded. "Thank God it doesn't change much. Because most of this is government land, building is strictly limited. And in the Cabinets, all motorized vehicles are restricted."

"Not even a motorcycle is allowed," Jordan said. "You have to use mountain bikes."

He cupped his hands to see through the wide windows of the cabin.

Rachel's neck ached from swiveling to appreciate the view. "What does the government do with all this land?"

"Some's set aside for campgrounds, wilderness hiking trails. Some is leased to logging companies that harvest the timber. Then the Forest Service replants. And it's a sanctuary for wildlife."

"Like bears?" Rachel shuddered.

"And deer, elk, moose, not to mention dozens of species of birds and small animals. See?" He pointed to a cluster of rocks directly below them. "Chipmunks."

"And over there, Dad." Jordan pointed a few feet away. "Ground squirrels."

"It's wonderful," Rachel said. "I can understand why you wouldn't want to live anywhere else."

"Want to see inside?" Wade asked.

Jordan shook his head. "It's padlocked."

Wade dug deep in his jeans pocket and pulled out a key. "The ranger from the Troy station dropped this off yesterday. Said we could spend the night in the cabin if we wanted."

"Wow, cool!" Jordan jumped up and down until Rachel could feel the tower swaying slightly beneath her feet.

Wade must have read the alarm on her face. "It's okay. The guy wires are rigged with some slack. Keeps the poles from snapping in a high wind."

He unlocked the padlock and opened the door. They stepped inside the fourteen-by-fourteen-foot room, but Rachel didn't feel crowded in the small space. Not with wall-to-wall windows opening onto the panoramic view. A built-in bed filled one corner. Another held a table and chairs. Along one wall stood a tiny gas cookstove. Nothing obstructed the view. In the center of the room was a waist-high pedestal topped with a round metal circle.

"What's this?" Rachel asked.

"A firefinder," Wade explained. "See the map? The tower is in the exact center. If there's a fire, the lookout can take an azimuth reading and call it in to the station. If another lookout gets a bead on the same fire, the ranger can pinpoint its exact location from where the readings cross."

Rachel looked around. "How could he call it in? There's no phone."

"When the tower was manned," Wade said, "the lookouts had two-way radios, their only connection with civilization for weeks at a time."

"Cool," Jordan said.

His father nodded. "But often lonely. Except for the occasional huckleberry pickers."

Rachel frowned. "But how did they live? There's no running water. No electricity."

Wade laughed. "Conditions were rough, but tolerable. Water was stored in galvanized cans at the foot of the tower. Propane tanks fueled the stove and the lamps. And the Forest Service delivered groceries every few weeks."

"Dad said they took baths in a washtub," Jordan said. He pointed toward a stand of trees near the road. "And the outhouse is down there."

Wade nodded. "My lookout friends called it 'the hundred-yard dash.'"

"Gosh," Jordan said, "no TV. No computer. Bummer."

"What did they do for fun?" Rachel asked.

Wade grinned. "Well, the lookouts I knew *were* honeymooners—"

"Don't go there," Rachel said with a shake of her head and a glance at Jordan.

Wade's expression sobered. "The lookouts had to be on alert all day. They kept a constant vigil for any sign of smoke. The earlier a fire was detected, the easier it was to control."

"And at night?" Rachel asked.

"If there were storms," Wade explained, "they

had to chart every lightning strike on the firefinder. Then they'd watch those spots for days to make sure a 'sleeper' didn't flare up.''

"Did they have to fight the fires?'' Jordan asked.

"Only if the fire was within hiking distance of the tower. Each lookout kept a smokechaser's pack on hand with pick, shovel and rations, just in case.''

Rachel sat cross-legged on the bed and gazed across to the snow-topped Cabinet Mountains. "Still, it must have been a wonderful way to spend the summer, being paid to live with this magnificent view.''

"And an even better way to spend a honeymoon.'' Wade's gaze met hers, and she flushed, remembering their kiss on the mountainside.

She wished she could remember more—remember her past. Then maybe she could make sense of the feelings tumbling inside her. She'd been enchanted by the Montana mountains. She couldn't love Jordan more if he were her own flesh and blood. And Wade? She wanted to love him, but every time he seemed to open up to her, he slammed a door shut in her face. If she allowed her feelings for him to flourish, would she end up with a broken heart? He'd warned her from the first that love wasn't part of the bargain he offered. But without love, how much of a bargain was it?

"Wow! Look at that!''

Jordan's exclamation interrupted her thoughts. The boy pointed to the southwest horizon. Dark anvil-shaped clouds dwarfed the mountains and glided closer, like battleships in formation.

"We're in for a storm," Wade said. "We'd better sit it out in the truck."

Jordan barely contained his excitement. "Aw, Dad, can't we watch from here? We can track the lightning strikes, just like the lookouts did."

Wade raised his eyebrows and looked at Rachel. "You afraid of lightning?"

Rachel had no past references to fall back on. "I don't know…"

"Please, Rachel," Jordan begged. "It won't hurt you. There's a lightning rod on the roof. And you can stand on the special stool."

The boy dragged a small stool with glass insulators on its feet from beneath the table. In spite of the ominous clouds and the rumble of distant thunder, Rachel couldn't deny Jordan his adventure. His eyes shone with excitement, and his slender body shivered with anticipation. Standing on tiptoe, at Wade's instruction he aimed the firefinder at the foremost cloud. A gigantic bolt of lightning zigzagged from the sky and struck a distant ridge.

"The ranch is gettin' blasted," Jordan said.

"Make a note of the strikes." Wade handed Jordan a pencil and notepad from his pocket. "We'll check those areas for sleepers in a few days."

Jordan aimed the firefinder toward the ranch and scrawled azimuth readings. "Wow, that one wasn't far from the barn."

Wade's gaze met Rachel's over the boy's head. She couldn't tell whether the light in his eyes was a glimmer of yearning or a flicker of light reflected from the lightning. Whatever the look had been, it disappeared as Wade bent over the map with his son and plotted lightning strikes. She was sure she hadn't imagined it. More than electricity had crackled in the air between them during that brief moment, but Wade seemed determined to ignore it.

Disappointed, she focused her attention on the weather raging outside and tried to ignore the whirlwind of emotions Wade triggered inside her.

The storm swept up the mountain and engulfed the tower in pounding rain, obscuring the view.

"Wow," Jordan said, "I counted twenty-three strikes."

"Will they all start fires?" Rachel asked, glad for a neutral topic.

"The rain will douse any surface fires," Wade explained. "It's the sleepers, the fires that burn in the hearts of trees for days until the wood dries out and the whole tree explodes, that will cause problems."

Unable now to track the lightning through the heavy downpour, Jordan sat on the bed and bounced a few times on the mattress, sending up a cloud of dust. "Can we sleep up here tonight, Dad?"

Rachel glanced at Wade in alarm. The tiny cabin had appeared spacious until the storm shrouded the view. Now, in the darkness, it seemed small. And intimate. With her emotions shifting faster than the winds that buffeted the tower, sleeping in such close proximity to the man at the center of her turmoil didn't seem such a good idea.

"What about your camping project?" Wade said. "Don't you have to sleep outdoors?"

"Yeah," Jordan said with a sheepish grin. "I forgot."

Rachel breathed a sigh of relief. Until her memory returned and she could sort out her feelings against that backdrop, she wanted to keep both physical and emotional distance from the all-too-enticing Wade Garrett.

Once the storm cleared, they descended the tower stairs. Wade and Jordan searched for firewood while Rachel unpacked the provisions Ursula had supplied for their supper. Wade returned with an armload of only slightly damp wood and soon had a fire roaring in a circle of stones on the mountaintop. Rachel helped Jordan dice carrots and potatoes and add them to chunks of beef they had simmering in an iron pot.

Near the fire was a large flat stone. Rachel covered it with a red-checkered cloth, and Jordan set out the plates. Wade disappeared for a few minutes, and when he returned, thrust a bouquet of colorful wildflowers he'd picked into her hands.

Rachel flushed with pleasure. "Thank—"

"Don't go getting the wrong idea," he said with a sharpness that made her wince.

"The wrong idea?"

"They're for a centerpiece. That's all. Don't be reading any more into it."

Confused, Rachel pondered the uncomfortable expression that failed to dull the handsomeness of Wade's rugged face. The man was a walking paradox. How could she determine how he felt about her when he didn't appear to know himself?

Jordan approached and eyed the flowers with disgust. "For Pete's sake, Dad, this is a campout, not some fancy dinner."

"They're *wild* flowers, so that makes them okay," Rachel assured the boy with a smile. She turned her back on Wade, placed the flowers in a large plastic cup, filled it with water and placed it in the center of the rock.

When she glanced at Wade again, he had gathered his composure and stopped looking like an awkward teenager at his first prom. "That's right, son. Part of camping is learning the fauna and flora. This pink flower here, for instance, is a wild rose. And these berries are chokecherries."

Still smarting from Wade's strange behavior, Rachel stirred the stew and watched as Wade and Jordan wandered down the ridge, identifying and discussing various plants. They were so alike, the boy a miniature version of the man, and she wondered fleetingly if she'd be around long enough to see Jordan grow as tall as his father. She'd have to make her mind up soon whether or not to accept Wade's unorthodox proposal. She couldn't remain forever in "houseguest" limbo at the ranch.

AFTER SUPPER, to Jordan's delight, Rachel declared the meal a success, the best stew she'd ever eaten.

"When did you last eat stew?" Wade teased.

"I can't remem—" She returned his grin. "But I can guarantee no stew was ever as good as Jordan's."

Wade winked at his son. "At least none of us has a bellyache. Not yet, anyway."

With his face lit up like Christmas, Jordan glowed with pleasure at his father's teasing.

After clearing away the plates, and pouring coffee

for the grown-ups, they settled back against rocks near the fire and looked to the north, scanning the sky for signs of the aurora borealis.

"Sometimes the northern lights can be spotted even this far south," Wade said. "See those rose-colored streaks? They'll show there after dark."

Rachel gazed at the black peaks silhouetted against the crimson sky, and sipped her coffee contentedly. She could choose a worse life, she thought, than spending the next ten years with Wade and Jordan Garrett. But could she choose a better one? And without her memory, how was she to tell?

"Anybody know a story?" Wade asked.

"Not stories," Jordan begged. "Tell Rachel your jokes, Dad."

Wade's dark eyes twinkled, and Rachel couldn't help noticing that his shoulders were as broad and sturdy at the boulder he leaned against. "There was this traveling salesman and a farmer's daughter—" he began.

"Wade!" Rachel lifted her eyebrows and glanced at Jordan in alarm.

"Just kidding," Wade said with a slow grin that weakened her knees and made her glad she was sitting down. "What kind of jokes do you want, half-pint?"

"Elephant jokes," Jordan insisted.

"Okay." Wade looked to Rachel. "Stop me if you've heard these."

She snuggled back against the rock, enjoying herself. "Now I know you're kidding. How would I remember?"

Wade laughed, a hearty sound, if somewhat rusty

from disuse. "One of the benefits of your amnesia. All jokes are fresh."

"Tell the joke, Dad."

"Do you know why elephants have flat feet?" Wade looked at Rachel expectantly.

She shook her head. "I have no idea."

"From jumping out of palm trees," Jordan answered with a giggle.

His laughter was infectious, and Rachel joined in.

"I have one," Jordan said. "How can you tell if elephants have been in your refrigerator?"

Wade looked puzzled, but from the glimmer in his eye, Rachel was certain he knew the answer. "Give up?" Jordan asked.

Wade and Rachel nodded.

"They leave footprints in the Jell-O."

The boy's silliness was contagious. Rachel laughed in spite of herself.

"I have another one," Wade said. "Not an elephant joke, but a riddle. What's big and purple and goes slam-slam-slam-slam?"

Jordan's forehead creased in thought. "What?"

"A four-door grape." Wade was warming to his role as jokemeister. For the first time since Rachel had met him, a burden seemed to have lifted from his shoulders.

"Tell another," Jordan begged when his giggles stopped.

Wade thought a moment. "What's big and black and dangerous and sits in a tree?"

"A bear?" Rachel guessed. With a shiver, she glanced around uneasily and drew closer to the fire.

"Good guess, but not the answer," Wade said.

"What's big and black and dangerous? A crow with a machine gun."

With dizzying effect, a remembered joke burst into her consciousness, but she couldn't recall its source. "I know one!"

Wade looked at her, puzzled. "You remember?"

"Uh-huh. It just popped into my head out of nowhere."

"Remember anything else?" Anxiety flickered in Wade's eyes.

Odd, Rachel thought. He looked as if he were *afraid* of her remembering. "What's your joke?" Jordan asked, still chuckling over the crow with the machine gun.

Rachel grinned at the boy. "What's big and green and dangerous?"

Wade and Jordan looked at each other and shrugged.

"A thundering herd of pickles!" She joined in their laughter, and the sound reverberated off the rocks across the valley. A full moon had risen over Snowshoe Peak and bathed the mountain meadow where they sat in cool, silver light.

"You're neat, Rachel," Jordan said when he'd caught his breath. "Are you going to be my mother?"

Wade grew still. Rachel held her own breath, waiting for him to speak, afraid of saying the wrong thing. Jordan, sensing he'd stepped over a forbidden line, tensed and gazed anxiously at his father.

"Rachel's just visiting with us for now, Jordan. You shouldn't ask personal questions." The disapproval in Wade's voice banished the warmth they had experienced with their ridiculous jokes. Jordan looked crushed, and Rachel had to restrain herself from reaching to hug him.

"Tell me about my mama," Jordan said to his father. He stuck his chin in the air, as if bracing for a blow. "How come you never talk about her?"

Realizing the boy was treading on even more dangerous ground, Rachel stiffened. Ursula had warned that nobody at the ranch spoke of Maggie. Yet here was Jordan, blundering through a potential mine field with his questions.

Pain etched Wade's face, and for a moment, Rachel feared he wouldn't answer the boy. With his gaze fixed on the eastern mountains, he said in a voice strangely devoid of emotion, "You know we don't talk about her."

Jordan's tight shoulders tensed a notch, but he plowed ahead bravely. "I've never even seen her picture. Did she look like me?"

A vein in Wade's temple throbbed as if in agony. He pushed himself quickly to his feet and ground out words between his teeth. "Don't ask anymore. I'm not answering."

He kicked a half-burned log deeper into the fire and stomped off into the darkness.

Jordan's face contorted with grief, and tears rolled down his cheeks. This time Rachel didn't resist the urge to pull him into her arms.

"He thinks I'm a sissy when I cry."

"Everybody needs a good cry now and then."

"He hates me," Jordan sobbed.

"No, he doesn't." She smoothed back the boy's hair and wiped his tears with her shirtsleeve. "When someone you love dies, sometimes the pain of that loss is so bad, it hurts to talk about it. Someday your dad will tell you what you want to know. When he's ready. Your father loves you.''

''Yeah,'' Jordan said with a sniff. ''How come he never says so?''

Rachel's heart wrenched for the boy, and she drew him closer. ''Maybe he just doesn't know how.''

Jordan pulled away and looked up at her with red-rimmed eyes. ''It's only three words. How hard can it be?''

The knot in her throat kept her from answering. She hugged him again until she regained her voice. ''It's late, and you've had a busy day. Better turn in.''

With head bowed and shoulders slumped, Jordan unrolled his sleeping bag and pulled off his boots. As he climbed between the down-filled covers, Rachel sat cross-legged beside him. ''I'll stay here until you fall asleep.''

''Rachel,'' he murmured in a voice still raspy with tears, ''I wish you were my mom.''

''Any woman would be proud to have you for a son, Jordan Garrett.'' She kissed his tear-streaked cheek and pulled the sleeping bag up under his chin. ''Sleep tight.''

She sat with him until his even breathing signaled a deep sleep. Rising to her feet on stiff legs, she dusted off her jeans and headed toward the ridge where Wade had disappeared. She found him sitting on a rock, staring at the stars.

"The boy needs to know about his mother," she said, prepared to do battle for Jordan.

"It's none of your business."

Anger flared deep inside, giving her courage. "Oh, but it is. If we're going to have a *business* arrangement where it's my *business* to act as Jordan's mother, then it's my *business* to see that he's happy."

Wade shifted uneasily on his rocky perch. "Why shouldn't he be happy? He has everything a child needs."

"He thinks you don't love him."

Wade reeled slightly, as if her words had been a blow. "Of course I love him!"

"Have you ever told him?"

"I don't have to. He should know without my saying it."

Rachel stared at him in disbelief. She wanted to shake him till he rattled. "Where did you get such a crazy notion?"

"My dad never said he loved me—"

"But don't you wish he had?"

Wade thought for a moment. "I can't imagine him ever saying the words. He was a hard, quiet man."

"Is that the way you want Jordan to remember you?"

Wade sighed. "No."

"Then tell him you love him. And tell him about his mother. He deserves to know."

Wade surged to his feet, towering over her. The pale moonlight illuminated the suffering on his face. "I don't talk about Maggie. Ever. Not to anyone."

He turned on his heel and tramped farther down the mountain, disappearing from sight. With a heavy heart, Rachel returned to the campsite. Jordan slept peacefully, oblivious of the exchange that had occurred between her and his father. Just as well, Rachel thought. The poor kid didn't need any more grief.

She tugged her sleeping bag from the bed of the pickup and spread it close to Jordan's near the fire. As she pulled off her boots, she considered her situation. Her memories hadn't returned. In truth, they might never return, so she couldn't wait for them to resurface before making a decision about accepting Wade's offer. If only Jordan weren't involved, she could decide in a heartbeat. The boy needed love and caring, and she had plenty of both for the child.

But the father? How could she remain in a strictly business relationship and live in the same house with a man who made her pulse race, who kept her feelings in such turmoil that half the time she wanted to kiss him, the other half to kick him? What kind of emotional hell would she be sentencing herself to if she agreed to Wade Garrett's bizarre proposal?

And how could she leave Jordan if she didn't?

The questions still buzzed in her head as she dropped off to sleep.

A CAR DOOR SLAMMED and footsteps sounded on the front walk. She ran through the tiny house toward the front entrance.

"Daddy's home," she yelled to her mother in the kitchen.

Standing on tiptoes, she turned the lock and pulled open the heavy door. "Hi, Daddy!"

The tall man in a gray business suit and red tie leaned down and swept her into his arms. "Jenny, pumpkin. What did you do today?"

"Mommy and me went shopping."

"Did you buy me something?"

Her face fell. "No. But Mommy bought me new shoes."

He whirled her through the air, and when he set her on her feet, her mother stood beside him, wearing her best dress and carrying her coat.

"We'll be back next week, Jennifer. Mrs. Cooper will take good care of you while we're gone."

Panic clawed at her throat. She couldn't let them leave. If they walked out that door, she knew they'd never return. She tried to scream, but couldn't make a sound.

The door slammed. They were gone.

She crumpled on the rug, sobbing, sobbing....

"Rachel? Rachel?"

Someone was shaking her shoulder. She awakened in her sleeping bag with Wade leaning over her.

"Are you all right?" She couldn't see his face in the darkness, but his tone was worried.

"I'm..." Her fingers touched her cheeks and came away wet with tears. "I'm fine. It was a bad dream, that's all."

"You're shaking." With one swift movement, he scooped her up, sleeping bag and all, and set her closer to the fire. When he had her settled, he threw on extra logs and stirred the coals with a branch.

She glanced toward Jordan. "I didn't waken him?"

Wade shook his head. "He's sawing logs so hard, he won't stir till morning."

With a graceful movement for such a big man, he folded his legs beneath him and sat beside her. "Your dream? Was it a memory?"

Rachel shrugged and pulled the sleeping bag tighter around her. The sorrow of the dream still held her in its grasp, and she fought to keep from weeping. "I don't know. I was a little girl with my mom and dad. They were leaving on a trip, and I knew if they left, they'd never come back."

"So it could have been a memory?" He studied her face as if looking for answers to a puzzle.

"I doubt it. This man was a businessman. You said my father was a farmer. And the woman in the dream called me Jennifer. It must have been one of those nonsensical dreams that mean nothing. But it made me sad."

She shivered. Wade moved toward her, placed his arm around her and pulled her close. He felt solid and strong, and smelled pleasantly of leather and sunshine. Giving in to impulse, she laid her head on his shoulder.

"Don't be sad, Rachel. I promise you, everything's going to work out fine."

She drifted off to sleep again with his voice ringing in her ears, remaining conscious only long enough to think he sounded as unhappy as she'd felt in her dream.

Chapter Nine

Wade tiptoed to the door of his study, opened it a crack and listened. He could hear Rachel and Jordan in the kitchen, telling Ursula about their camping trip while the housekeeper prepared lunch.

With the coast clear, he closed the door, hurried to his desk and phoned the sheriff's office.

"Any luck with those fingerprints?" he asked when Dan Howard came on the line.

"Couldn't find a match. But at least you know she isn't a wanted criminal."

Biting back disappointment, Wade snorted. "Anyone with half a brain would know that after being around Rachel only a few minutes." His tone sobered. "But that doesn't help my situation. I have to know who she is."

"I don't have much to go on. Can't you give me any other clues?"

Wade recalled Rachel's account of her dream the night before on Keeler Mountain. "Her first name could be Jennifer, but I'm not sure."

"Well, that's a start. I'll check the railroad's passenger list."

Wade raked his fingers through his hair in frustration. "I know you're busy, man, but can you make it quick? Things are getting complicated here."

Dan laughed. "With a woman as pretty as Rachel, they always do."

Wade hung up the phone and swiveled his desk chair toward the window. Across the lawn, he could view the neatly painted barn and bunkhouse, and beyond, surrounded by secure fencing, cattle grazing on the tall grass sweetened by recent rain. The idyllic scene usually calmed him, but not today. Every time he recalled Rachel falling asleep last night in his arms, his pulse speeded up, his blood heated and any sense of peacefulness went south.

He needed time. And distance. He was already doing all he could to discover her real identity. And with no place for her to go, he couldn't send her away.

Not that he wanted to.

It saddened him to think of the day when either she would remember or Dan would discover who she was, and she would return to her own people. The house would seem empty without her. Wade's arms already missed holding her after last night.

A knock sounded at his door, scattering his thoughts.

"Come in."

Ursula slipped inside quietly and closed the door behind her. "Well?"

Wade shook his head. "Still no news. In her dreams someone called her Jennifer. Dan's checking it out."

Ursula folded her hands in her apron and fixed him with her no-nonsense stare. He'd squirmed under that look many times as a boy, and it took a manly effort to keep from squirming now.

"You have to tell her," the housekeeper said. "Ain't fair for her to go on thinking she's someone she ain't."

"I know, but the doctor says until we can tell her who she really *is*, the shock may prevent her from ever remembering. I wouldn't want that to happen."

Ursula's dark eyes glimmered, reminding Wade of a hawk swooping for the kill. "You going to marry her?"

He pushed to his feet and shoved his hands in his pockets to keep from breaking something to ease his stress. "How can I? For all we know, she's married already."

"And if you find out she isn't?"

Wade couldn't unscramble his feelings about Rachel, but even if he could, he wasn't discussing them with Ursula. "Any sign of Larry Crutchfield while we were gone?"

She grimaced to acknowledge he'd sidestepped her question. "Lefty said Crutchfield drove by real slow in his blue Mercedes yesterday afternoon, but when he spotted Lefty at the gate with his gun, he speeded up and disappeared." Her white eyebrows knotted. "You think he'll come back?"

Wade nodded. "Wouldn't be surprised. He seemed the tenacious type. I don't want him upsetting Rachel."

"And what about Jordan?"

"What about him?"

"He's grown powerful fond of that woman. How's he gonna take it when she leaves?"

Wade shoved his fingers through his hair again. "He'll get over it."

Ursula skewered him with a look that made him squirm in spite of himself. "Like he got over losing his mother?"

Wade's temper flared, but before he could reply, she was halfway out the door.

"Lunch is on the table," she called over her shoulder.

With a sigh of resignation, Wade followed her into the kitchen.

He couldn't help thinking of the irony of the scene of domestic tranquility that greeted him. Whistling happily under his breath, his face and hands scrubbed pink, Jordan set the table. At the stove, Rachel held earthenware bowls while Ursula ladled homemade soup into them. The mouthwatering aroma of baking bread filled the room. Under different circumstances, the sight would have lifted his spirits and had him whistling with Jordan. For now, he fought sudden indigestion.

"Sit and eat," Ursula ordered. "Ain't nothing worse'n cold soup."

They took their places while Ursula removed a round loaf of brown bread from the oven and sliced it into steaming wedges.

Jordan attacked his soup as if he hadn't eaten three eggs and half a pound of bacon for breakfast on the mountain. He stopped long enough to point to the counter beside the stove. "That for dessert?"

Wade noted the foot-high cake glistening with chocolate frosting.

"That is my five-layer chocolate cake for the barn dance." Ursula shook the bread knife at Jordan. "And I better not find any boy's fingerprints in it when we get there."

Rachel smiled at Jordan with a tenderness that wrenched Wade's heart. "If you're still hungry after lunch, there're sugar cookies in the pantry."

She turned to Wade. "Ursula says there's a buffet supper before the dance, so we'll be frying chicken this afternoon to take with us."

Wade was glad for the neutral topic. "What about the huckleberries we picked?"

"Ursula put them in the freezer," Rachel said. "We'll make jelly on Monday."

If you're still here Monday, he thought sadly, wondering how soon Dan Howard would discover her true identity. The sooner the better. The longer she stayed, the harder Wade would find letting her go.

"Do I have to go to the barn dance?" Jordan asked.

He looked at his son in surprise. "Don't you want to? All your friends will be there."

"Yeah, but it's at Spider Woman's place."

"Spider Woman?" Rachel asked.

"Sue Ann Swenson," Jordan said with a grimace.

"Miss Swenson," Wade corrected him.

Rachel smiled at the boy. "Why do you call her Spider Woman?"

"'Cause she gives me the creeps." Jordan wiped his mouth on his napkin. "May I be excused?"

Struggling to keep a stern expression, Wade nodded. Ursula turned her face to the stove, but her shoulders shook.

Jordan raced out of the kitchen, braked to a halt and returned to the pantry. He reappeared a few seconds later with a handful of cookies and darted into the hall.

"I swear, since you arrived, Rachel," Ursula said, "that boy's been eating like there's no tomorrow."

Wade groaned inwardly at Ursula's choice of words. Jordan had no idea how limited Rachel's tomorrows at the ranch were.

Ursula poured herself a cup of coffee, sat in Jordan's deserted chair and eyed Wade. "Well, don't you think you'd better tell her?"

Wade tensed and glanced from Ursula to Rachel in alarm. Surely his housekeeper didn't intend to reveal Rachel's false identity?

"Tell me what?" Rachel asked.

"About Sue Ann Swenson." Ursula sipped her coffee, her gaze on Wade over the rim of her cup.

Wade felt a fleeting moment of relief, replaced by irritation. "What about Sue Ann?"

Ursula grunted. "Jordan's not far off with his Spider Woman nickname. Although I'd say Cat Woman is closer to the mark. That predatory female has sharp claws and a tongue like a razor. Ain't all her fault. She was an only child. Her parents spoiled her rotten. Let her do and say anything she damned well pleased."

Rachel looked puzzled, but Wade wasn't about to enlighten her. He had enough troubles without dragging Sue Ann Swenson into the mix.

Ursula, evidently, had no such reservations. "Ever since Mag—" she swallowed the rest of the forbidden name "—since Wade became a widower, Sue Ann's had her cap set for him."

Rachel's green eyes twinkled. "He *is* an attractive man."

"Don't talk about me like I'm not here," he growled, but inwardly he was pleased. Much good it would do him, her thinking him attractive. Not with the possibility of an unidentified husband waiting in the wings.

"Wade's looks ain't got that much to do with it," Ursula said. "Sue Ann's not long on sentiment. She's more interested in profit."

"Profit?" Rachel asked.

Ursula nodded and drained her coffee cup. "The Swenson place shares a boundary with this one. If the two properties were joined, they'd form one of the biggest holdings in northwest Montana. Sue Ann would be a very wealthy and influential woman."

"Interesting," Rachel said, "but it's nothing to do with me."

"Oh, no?" Ursula plunked her cup down with a thud. "That woman'll make your life hell if she views you as a threat to her plans."

"Rachel's no threat—" Wade bit off his words too late. They'd hit home with an impact, judging by the surprised look on Rachel's face.

Looking embarrassed, she rose from the table. "If you'll excuse me—"

Wade stopped her with a hand on her arm. "Don't go taking what I said the wrong way. You're not a threat because I'm not interested in Sue Ann Swenson.''

"I only brought Sue Ann up," Ursula said, "so her catty comments won't catch you by surprise, Rachel."

"Thanks." Rachel flushed the attractive pale pink of a Montana wild rose and began gathering dirty dishes. "I'll help you clean up, Ursula."

Wade, afraid of sticking his foot in his mouth again, pushed to his feet. "I have chores. Damn good lunch, Ursula."

He retreated to the barn as fast as his boots would carry him.

RACHEL LOADED THE LAST of the bowls in the dishwasher and closed the door.

At the sink, Ursula wiped her hands on a dish towel. "You're awful quiet. Don't let what I said about Sue Ann bother you. Wade's got no use for her."

Rachel forced a smile. "It isn't that."

"I know sad when I see it. What's bothering you, girl?"

Rachel shook her head. "Nothing."

The housekeeper gave her a compassionate look. "You've been through a rough patch, hurt in that train wreck, losing your memory. Things must seem all topsy-turvy. If you want to talk, I'm a good listener."

Rachel hugged Ursula and blinked back tears at the older woman's caring. "I can't talk about my feelings until I sort them out. Unless you're ready to fry chicken now, I'll take a walk. Maybe exercise and fresh air will clear my head.''

"Go ahead. I always have a lie-down after lunch. These old bones don't have as much get up and go as they used to.''

Rachel laughed. "You have enough energy to run circles around me.''

Ursula chuckled. "Leo'll tell you I run on high-octane orneriness. Now, take your walk. It'll do you good.''

Rachel strode through the quiet house and out the front door. The rich perfume of rambler roses blended with the resinous scent of pine, a heady mixture that lifted her sagging spirits. She skipped down the broad front steps and headed down the long drive that led to the highway.

Although it had only been a few days since she'd first ridden up that road with Wade, she felt as if she'd been in Montana all her life. She'd fallen in love with the wide curve of deep blue sky and the sheltering bulk of green mountain ranges that hugged the valley. The ranch house seemed like home, and Ursula and Leo seemed like family.

Not to mention Jordan and Wade. She'd grown more than fond of both of them. Too fond. Leaving them would break her heart, but she wasn't sure Wade wanted her to stay. One minute he acted as if he cared about her, the next she was suffering frostbite from his coldness. His seesaw reactions exhausted her, leaving her wary and wondering how he was going to respond next.

She tramped steadily along the tree-lined drive until she reached the entrance to the ranch at the highway. Lefty Starr perched on the top rail of the fence by the gate, cradling a rifle in his arms. A large No Trespassing sign was tacked prominently to the fence post.

As she approached, the blond cowhand smiled and tipped his hat. "Nice day, ma'am."

"Beautiful." She nodded toward the rifle. "Expecting trouble?"

His toothy smile faltered, but only for an instant. "No, ma'am. I just keep this—" he patted the rifle "—for timber rattlers. Better watch your step. Never know when you might stumble on one."

"Thanks for the warning."

Rachel turned back toward the ranch. If Lefty was guarding the gate against snakes, she'd eat her boots. Whatever or whoever he was looking for, nobody seemed inclined to tell her.

She was dealing with too many unanswered questions, not even counting her missing memories. It was time she and Wade Garrett had a serious heart-to-heart talk. She needed straight answers, and by the time she'd hiked back to the ranch house, she'd figured out how to get them.

She headed for the barn and entered the cool, dark interior.

When her eyes had adjusted to the darkness, she noted the stalls that lined the walls, all empty of horses, except two. From the shadows, a dark-eyed palomino and a docile bay mare stared back at her and snuffled gently. The pungent odor of horse manure blended with the fresh scent of hay.

She found Wade at the far end of the barn, mucking out a stall. He hadn't heard her approach, and silently she watched him, stripped to the waist, the hard muscles of his arms and shoulders bunching as he lifted his pitchfork and tossed its load into a small cart. Sweat glistened on his tanned skin, and his mahogany-colored hair fell over his forehead into his eyes. His jaw locked and eyes burning, he attacked the dirty hay as if it were a mortal enemy.

She figured there ought to be law against any man looking so darned handsome. "Don't the hands do that?"

"Most of the time." He barely broke his rhythm as he transferred another load of muck to the cart. Without looking at her, he continued working. "I like doing it. Helps me think."

"I've been thinking, too."

This time he rammed the pitchfork into the cart. He jerked a bandanna from his back pocket, mopped his face and met her gaze. "Sounds serious."

"It is." Unnerved by his dark stare, she plunged ahead before she lost her courage. "Can we talk?"

He turned abruptly, grabbed his shirt from the stall railing and stomped out the barn's rear door.

"Thought we agreed you'd wait till you get your memories back," he called over his shoulder.

She hurried to catch up and almost ran into him when he stopped suddenly at a bench outside the door. "It's been weeks since the accident. What if they never return?"

For a split second he stood absolutely still. Then he plunged his head into a trough of water on the bench. When he straightened, he sluiced water from his hair, scrubbed his hands with soap and, after rinsing them, reached for a nearby towel.

She fought off the desire to take the towel and dry him off herself. Her unexpected hunger for intimacy made their talk even more necessary.

"Remember the day I left the hospital?" she said. "I asked that we not discuss your marriage proposal again until I was ready."

He stopped rubbing his chest with the towel, but he didn't meet her gaze. "I remember."

"I'm ready now to discuss it."

"Well, I'm not." He slung the towel on the bench and pulled on his shirt.

His refusal caught her by surprise. "But—"

He still avoided meeting her eyes. "I have several miles of fence to check before sundown."

Frustration boiled within her. She hadn't worked up her courage only to be stymied by his rebuff. "Fine. I'll go with you."

For the first time, he looked her in the eye. "You know how to ride?"

She couldn't remember whether she'd ever ridden a horse. "Can't you take the pickup?"

"And tear up good grassland?" He shook his head. "If you won't go on horseback, guess our little chat'll have to wait a day or two."

He headed back toward the barn.

She stepped in his path and crossed her arms over her chest. "No."

Towering over her, he lifted his eyebrows in surprise. "No?"

Stunned by her own boldness, she stammered, "I—I don't want to wait. I want things settled."

He sighed and shook his head. "Why are you in such an all-fired hurry all of a sudden?"

She gazed up at him. "It's bad enough my past is in limbo. I want my future settled."

His expression softened. Reaching out, he stroked her cheek with the back of his work-callused hand. "No one knows the future, Rachel. All any of us have is today."

The sadness in his voice touched her, made her want to wrap her arms around him and never let go. She shook away the longing. All the more reason to find out where she stood.

"Please, can't we talk now?"

Mischief glinted in his dark eyes. "If you want to ride fences with me."

"Ride?" She swallowed hard. If she refused, it might be days before she'd have another chance to confront him.

He nodded toward the barn. "Molly's a nice, gentle mare. Good for a beginner."

"You said I grew up on a farm. I've probably ridden before."

A strange expression flashed across his face before it settled into neutral lines again. "Probably."

"Molly it is, then," she said with a boldness she hoped she wouldn't regret.

She followed him into the barn and watched as he saddled the palomino, then Molly. For a gentle horse, the mare had an excess of energy, prancing and turning while Wade cinched the saddle. He led the animals out of the barn, and Rachel followed, eyeing the spirited Molly warily.

Wade must have noticed her reluctance. "Change your mind?"

She wanted to back out, but that would mean

waiting for their talk. She shook her head. "Help me up."

Placing her left foot in the stirrup, she tossed her right leg over Molly's back, all too aware of the warm, firm pressure of Wade's palms on her backside, boosting her into the saddle. The mare skittered backward, and Rachel almost slid off the other side. Struggling to maintain her dignity, she righted herself and grabbed the reins.

Not bothering to conceal his amusement, Wade swung onto the palomino with an ease and grace that made her feel all the more clumsy by comparison.

"We'll start off slow," he said. "Give you a chance to get accustomed to Molly."

Rachel smiled, refusing to let her nervousness show. If Wade was reluctant to discuss his proposal, he'd found a perfect way to distract her. She'd already anticipated a hard time choosing what she wanted to say. Concentrating on staying on Molly made conversation a whole lot tougher.

She gripped the mare's body with her knees and followed Wade's palomino at a slow walk toward the pasture.

"You're doing great," he said with an encouraging grin. "Let's step up the pace."

Before she could protest, Wade clucked his tongue, nudged his horse with his knees, and the big palomino broke into a trot. Molly followed suit, and Rachel soon found herself hanging on for dear life, gritting her teeth to keep from biting her tongue with each jolt, and praying her backbone wouldn't bounce through her brain.

"Relax," Wade called to her. "Pretend you're part of the horse."

She grimaced at him. She felt a part of the horse, all right. The hind part. Especially when she spied the dirt road running parallel to the pasture on the other side of the fence. Wade could have taken the pickup without spoiling his grassland. He just hadn't wanted to.

Pulling hard on Molly's reins, Rachel persuaded the mare to stop.

Wade, realizing she was no longer keeping pace, wheeled the stallion and returned. "What's wrong?"

"Nothing that a few minutes of straight talk won't solve."

Wade shifted uneasily in the saddle. "But my fences—"

"They'll keep." She took a deep breath to cool her temper. Anger wouldn't gain her the answers she wanted. "About your marriage proposal. I've thought it through and—"

"Mr. Garrett!"

A frantic shout floated across the pasture. Riding toward them as if outrunning the devil was a man Rachel recognized as one of Wade's hands. The rider drew opposite them and reined in his well-lathered horse.

"You're needed at the river," the hand said.

Wade pushed back his Stetson. "What's the trouble, Buck?"

The big man wiped his face with his sleeve, and Rachel noted he and his horse were splattered with mud.

"Rob's horse stumbled into a bog," Buck said. "It's up to its withers in mud, and we can't get her out."

"And Rob?" Wade asked.

"He's okay, but chest-high in mud, too. He won't leave her."

"Did you call the vet?"

Buck nodded. "Leo's with us. He rang Doc Heywood on his cell phone, and he's on his way."

Wade glanced at Rachel. "Can you make it back to the barn by yourself?"

She slid out of the saddle and grabbed the reins. "I'll lead Molly back. It's not that far."

Wade nodded. "Have Jordan help you with the saddle. I'll be back soon as I can."

He turned his horse. Buck joined him and the pair galloped toward the river.

With mounting frustration, Rachel watched them until they disappeared into the trees. She'd intended to confront Wade ever since lunch, to tell him she wanted to accept his proposal. What she was most anxious for, however, wasn't the telling but his reaction. His demeanor toward her had run hot and cold for the last two days, and she'd hoped her acceptance would force him to acknowledge how he felt about her.

This afternoon, he'd stalled her on purpose, and that fact made her uneasy. If he was still disposed toward going through with their marriage deal, why wasn't he willing to talk to her about it? From all she'd learned of him, she knew Wade Garrett was an honorable man. Was he going to tell her he'd changed *his* mind?

He kept saying she needed to delay a decision about marrying him until her memories returned. Was that what he was waiting for? For her to remember her past, so he could negate their agreement and send her back to her old life?

Her head ached from unanswered questions and the jostling Molly had given her. She was no closer to knowing where she stood than she'd been that morning.

With a sad heart, she turned toward the ranch.

Chapter Ten

Three hours later, Wade trudged up the stairs to his bedroom. Every bone in his body ached, and every inch of him was covered in mud. Between Rachel's insistence on discussing their marriage arrangement and Rob's stranded horse, he'd had enough crises for one day. Yet somehow he couldn't shake the feeling that something else was about to go wrong. Trouble always came in threes.

In his bathroom, he stripped off his muddy clothes and stepped into a hot shower. If he hurried, they wouldn't be too late for supper before the barn dance.

He scrubbed shampoo into his hair and shuddered. Sue Ann Swenson could qualify for the day's third disaster. He hoped she'd save her catty comments for him and leave Rachel alone, but, knowing Sue Ann, he realized that was asking too much of fate.

Ah, Rachel. What am I going to do with you?

Although he wouldn't have wished Rob's horse trouble on anybody, he'd been grateful for the interruption this afternoon. He had no idea what Rachel had been prepared to tell him, but no matter what her decision, it wouldn't have been good.

If she'd decided not to marry him and to return to her old life, she would find out all too quickly that she wasn't who she thought she was.

Even worse, if she'd decided to accept his proposal, he would either have to find some way to stall her or flat-out turn her down. He couldn't go marrying a woman who might already have a husband.

No matter how much Jordan liked her.

No matter how beautiful she was.

No matter how good she made him feel.

No matter how much he wanted to take her in his arms and kiss her until—

He turned off the hot water and blasted himself with a freezing cold spray, cursing the day he'd come up with his harebrained scheme for a wife. He'd once thought he couldn't find himself in a greater mess than Maggie had made of his life.

He'd been wrong. Today proved it.

Shivering, he shut off the shower and reached for a towel. His only hope was to stall Rachel long enough for the sheriff to discover her identity.

But how?

No answers came to him as he dressed for the dance. If he could draw Ursula aside during the evening, maybe she'd have an idea.

Stepping into the hall, he yelled to Jordan, "Let's go, son. We're already late," and bounded down the stairs. The sight that greeted him at the bottom drew him up short.

Rachel waited on a bench by the front door. The late afternoon sun streamed through the window panels and cast a golden glow over her blond hair. The green gingham dress she'd bought in town looked even more alluring than when she'd first tried it on, and he had to thrust his hands in his pockets to keep from reaching for her.

At his approach, she looked up and smiled with a sweetness that took his breath away. Then he noted the hint of cunning in her expression, and his stomach sank to his boots.

"Jordan went ahead with Leo and Ursula," she said. "That'll give us time to talk on the way."

Silently cursing his luck, Wade painted on an accommodating grin. "Then we'd better get going. Sue Ann doesn't take kindly to stragglers."

Hoping to head off her discussion, he began talking as soon as he started the pickup. "Leo tell you about the rescue?"

She shook her head. "Ursula had him loading food for the buffet. Did you save Rob's horse?"

"Eventually. We tried pulling her out by hand and then with the tractor. When that didn't work, the vet rigged a harness, and Dan Howard had the sheriff's department's helicopter flown in to lift the horse out."

Dan had watched the operation with Wade. "Found three Jennifers on the passenger list," the sheriff had told him. "We're in the process of tracking them down. Should have some answers for you soon."

"Is she all right?" Rachel asked.

Wade snapped his attention back to the present. "The horse? She's exhausted, but she'll be okay. It was a close call."

They rode in silence for a few minutes. Wade's mind raced, searching for safe topics of conversation. No woman except Maggie had ever had him in such a quandary.

Maggie.

Thank God, he thought, and grasped at the solution to his trouble.

"Rachel?"

"Yes?"

She smelled of fresh air, flowers and fragrant soap, and he struggled to keep his mind on what he had to say. "I know you want to discuss our marriage arrangement."

He caught her surprised expression from the corner of his eye.

"Heaven knows, I've tried," she said. "I've decided you're avoiding the topic."

"I have been," he said with sincerity, "but not for the reasons you might think."

At least part of his statement was true, he assured himself. She had no idea of the real explanation why he couldn't discuss their future.

"Then you haven't changed your mind?"

He could feel her glance at him, but he didn't dare meet her gaze. One look into those eyes as green as alpine meadow grass and he'd give himself away. "No, I haven't changed my mind."

"Then what's the problem?"

Taking a deep breath, he plunged ahead. "I don't think you have all the facts you need to make the right decision."

She sat motionless, staring out her window at the

passing grassland, glowing golden beneath the setting sun.

"It's still a business arrangement?" she asked in a neutral tone.

"Of course."

"You've explained the terms. I've met Jordan, seen the ranch. What else do I need to know?"

Wade steered with one hand and raked the other through his hair. "You don't know about Maggie."

She turned to him with an ironic smile. "It isn't as if I haven't tried. No one will talk about her."

"For good reason. When you hear, you'll understand."

She twisted toward him. "So tell me."

"Not now."

She heaved a sigh of frustration. "Why—"

"It's a long story, and we're almost to the Swensons'." He turned the pickup off the highway onto the Swenson ranch's access road. "We'll talk tomorrow."

"Promise?"

"Scout's honor." He raised three fingers and shot her a grin, feeling as if a boulder had been lifted from his chest. If he could delay her another day with Maggie's story, maybe the sheriff would have her real identity by then.

As Wade pulled up beneath a Douglas fir down the lane from the Swenson's barn, however, his sense of oppression returned. He'd been so concerned with stalling Rachel's decision making, he'd thrust Sue Ann Swenson clean out of his mind. The last thing he wanted was his marriage-hungry neighbor making trouble for Rachel.

He circled the truck and opened Rachel's door.

She hesitated before taking his hand and stepping out. "This is all new to me."

Wade tucked her hand through his arm and headed past the rows of parked trucks and sport utility vehicles toward the barn. "Just stick with me. I'll show you the ropes."

THE SOUNDS OF LIVELY conversation and laughter drifted down the lane. As they circled the low, modern ranch house, Rachel caught sight of the crowd in front of the barn.

Women were arranging food on trestle tables made from long planks and sawhorses. Nearby, steaks sizzled on a huge outdoor grill. Bales of hay, placed strategically around the yard, served as seats. Several children ran through the crowd, chasing a border collie, and a group of men, beers in hand, gathered by the fence. From inside the barn drifted the sounds of the band warming up for the dance after supper. Electric lights covered by paper lanterns had been strung across the yard, lighting the entire scene like a stage.

"It looks like fun." Rachel smiled up at Wade.

He ducked his head and whispered in her ear. "Here comes trouble. Don't let her fluster you."

Sue Ann Swenson was striding across the yard toward them. She wore white jeans that fit like paint and a red silk shirt, opened low to reveal her cleavage. Her gaze flitted over Rachel and rested on Wade with a hungry look.

"I was wondering when you'd show up," she said. "I've been waiting for you."

"We had a little horse trouble this afternoon," Wade said evenly. "Sorry we're late."

Ignoring Rachel, Sue Ann fanned her eyelashes at Wade. "You're a sight worth waiting for."

"You remember Rachel?"

Rachel forced herself to smile as she met Sue Ann's hostile stare. The woman, after all, was her hostess. "Looks like a wonderful party."

Sue Ann's dark eyes raked her from head to foot. "What a *quaint* outfit."

Wade pulled Rachel closer to his side. Reassured by his presence, she didn't let her smile waver. "I'm glad you like it."

"I didn't say I liked it," Sue Ann purred liked a predatory feline. "I've never gone in much for *Beverly Hillbillies* fashion."

Rachel fixed her eyes on Sue Ann's ample cleavage and grinned. "I prefer it to Frederick's of Hollywood."

Wade coughed, as if swallowing a laugh.

Sue Ann's eyes blazed. Evidently unable to think of a snappy comeback, she shifted her attention back to Wade. Tracing her bloodred nails down the sharp angle of his face, she crooned, "You'll save some dances for me, won't you?"

Rachel watched Wade stiffen beneath Sue Ann's touch. Couldn't the woman tell she wasn't wanted?

"You know I'm not a dancing man, Sue Ann."

Sue Ann leaned closer, her voluptuous lips inches from Wade's ear, and whispered seductively, but loudly enough for Rachel to hear. "You don't have to dance. We'll just hold each other while the music plays."

Wade took a step back, drawing Rachel with him. "You have other guests, Sue Ann. Rachel and I shouldn't monopolize the hostess."

His tone was friendly, but Rachel recognized the tension beneath his words. Sue Ann had to be deaf not to notice, but she seemed undeterred. "I'll be back," she promised, "for that dance."

"Don't hold your breath," Wade muttered, and wheeled Rachel toward the buffet table.

"The woman obviously upsets you," Rachel said. "Why don't you tell her to back off?"

"Sue Ann?" Wade shook his head. "Kicking doesn't get you anywhere with that woman unless you're a mule."

Rachel frowned. "Huh?"

"When Sue Ann sets her mind to something, can't anybody change it, so talking to her would be as effective as shouting at a post. The best I can do is avoid her."

Ursula joined them at the table and handed each an empty plate. "How'd it go with Sue Ann?"

"Coulda been worse," Wade said, "but Rachel held her own like a champion. First time I've ever seen Sue Ann struck speechless."

"I was watching," Ursula said. "Sue Ann's after you, son. It's as plain as red paint. And she won't take kindly to Rachel standing in her way."

"That kind of talk'll spoil a man's appetite." Wade motioned Rachel into the buffet line. "Let's eat before the Spider Woman returns."

The conspiratorial look he shot Rachel warmed her to her toes and washed away the bad taste Sue Ann had left in her mouth. Suddenly she was starving, especially with the aromas of grilled steak and hot bread wafting on the breeze.

While she filled her plate, Wade introduced her to his other neighbors. Several commented on how good it was to see him, making Rachel wonder how long it had been since Wade had attended a social function.

"Pleased to meetcha, Ms. O'Riley," Ken Johannson, a plump, red-faced man in his fifties, said. "I own the spread north of the Longhorn." He pointed to a large Blue Willow bowl on the buffet table. "Be sure to try Irma's hot potato salad. She's famous for it."

Wade wandered farther down the table, and Rachel dished a dollop of Iris's specialty onto her plate.

"How're you liking Montana?" Ken asked.

"It's beautiful, breathtaking." Rachel was warming to Wade's congenial neighbor. "And the people are certainly friendly."

"Plan to stay awhile?"

"I don't know," Rachel said. "Depends on how things work out."

Ken bent toward her and whispered, "Don't let Sue Ann Swenson run you off, you hear? Wade needs a good woman like you."

With a friendly wink, Ken moved down the line.

Rachel looked up to see Wade had returned, and she wondered if he'd heard Ken Johannson's advice. Wade's detached expression gave her no clue to what he was thinking, however.

She finished filling her plate and joined Jordan, Ursula, and Leo. Wade lifted a hay bale and moved it closer so they could all sit together.

Ursula tapped her foot in time with the music drifting from the barn. "Eat up, Leo. You'll need your strength for the Texas two-step."

The old foreman groaned. "After the day I've had, my feet feel as if they've wintered on a hard pasture. You'll have to find a younger man for a partner."

Ursula gaped at him in surprise. "Never known you to miss a dance, even if your feet were on fire. You ain't coming down with something?"

"Yup." Leo grinned back at her. "Old age."

As she dug into her steak, Rachel enjoyed the good-natured banter between the couple, but a glance across the barnyard spoiled her appetite.

Sue Ann was mingling with her guests, but her gaze often settled on Wade. When she caught Rachel's eye, she glared pure poison.

"Wow," Jordan said beside her. "If looks could kill, you'd be deader'n a fence post, Rachel."

If looks could kill.

Ray's mother was staring at her across the patio. Ray's dad was cooking chicken on the barbecue.

She handed Ray a glass of iced tea and whispered, "Why is your mother looking at me like that?"

"Don't take it personally, Jen. You know how much she wants grandchildren. She's tired of waiting for us to start our family."

Sinking into an Adirondack chair beside his, she folded her legs beneath her. "And you? What do you think?"

He grinned, flashing the smile that at one time had made her heart stutter and her knees weak. "We'll have a family when I'm ready. Not before."

"Don't I have any say in the matter?"

Ray patted her knee as if she were a child. "We've been over this a hundred times, Jen. The husband is the head of the family, so I make all the important decisions."

She wriggled uncomfortably in her chair. "Since children will be primarily my responsibility, seems like I should have some input in the arrangement."

Ray's smile disappeared, and his jaw hardened. "What kind of a wife are you? No wonder Mother disapproves."

For once her anger overcame her fear. "And you disapprove of me, too?"

He smiled again, but it didn't reach his eyes. "Not as long as you do as I say."

Fighting back tears, she rose from her chair, skirted the patio without glancing at her in-laws, and entered the house.

Once her refuge, her home now felt like a prison. She had to escape, but she had nowhere to go....

"Rachel? You okay?"

Jordan's voice jerked her back to the present.

His face was taut with worry. "Don't let ole Sue Ann spook you. Dad won't let her hurt you."

"What?" Rachel struggled to regain her bearings.

She hadn't been sleeping, so what she'd just experienced couldn't have been a dream.

It had to have been a memory.

She was married.

Unhappily married.

Was that why she'd agreed to accept Wade's crazy proposal? To get away from Ray, her insensitive, overbearing husband?

"Rachel?" Jordan slipped his hand into hers.

She squeezed the boy's fingers and forced a smile. "I'm fine, really. Just woolgathering."

She lifted her head. Wade, sitting on the hay bale opposite her, laid down his knife and fork and studied her with a puzzled expression.

"You seemed a thousand miles away," he said.

She took a deep breath and sidestepped the truth. "This is my first social event since the accident. Takes some getting used to."

"I thought maybe you were remembering something," Wade stated with a probing look.

Avoiding his eyes, Rachel set her plate aside. "If you'll excuse me, I need to visit the ladies' room."

"Inside the ranch house," Ursula said. "First door on the right."

To escape their questioning glances, Rachel hurried away from the crowd in the yard, a thousand questions of her own battering her.

What kind of woman was she?

Divorced?

Runaway wife?

Why hadn't she told Wade the truth in her letters?

How could she accept his proposal without knowing the answers? And how could she uncover the truth without alerting Wade to her deception?

She scurried up the steps of the house to the darkness of the porch, shaded from the light by climbing vines. Collapsing in a rush-seated rocker, she pressed her hands together to stop their trembling.

For the first time since regaining consciousness after her accident, she had lost her sense of self. Not that she'd remembered any of her previous life, but she'd at least always known her values, her instinct for right and wrong. She'd been comfortable with who she was.

Now she wasn't so sure.

How could she be? She didn't know herself any longer. Not if her memories were accurate.

She recalled Dr. Sinclair at the hospital. Tomorrow she could ride into Libby and visit her. The doctor might be able to tell her if her mind was playing tricks on her as a result of her accident.

Her entire body trembled. Dear God, what would she do if her memories were real?

Murmuring voices signaled people approaching, and Rachel drew deeper into the shadows of the porch.

"Looks like you've lost out where Wade Garrett is concerned," an unfamiliar female voice said with a note of triumph. "He seemed very preoccupied with the pretty woman he brought to the dance tonight."

"Don't count me out yet." Rachel recognized Sue Ann's aggressive tone. "As long as he hasn't married the little tramp, I'm still in the running."

"Tramp?" the other woman said with a note of interest. "Do you know something about this Rachel O'Riley you're not telling us?"

"Oh, please," another woman begged, "give us all the gossip, Sue Ann. Especially the juicy stuff."

"I haven't found anything yet," Sue Ann said, "but I have a private investigator looking into Miss O'Riley's past even as we speak."

"Just because he's looking doesn't mean he'll

find anything," the first woman said, sounding disappointed. "She looks ordinary enough to me."

"I'm not worried," Sue Ann said. "Everyone has dirt in their past if you dig deep enough. And believe me, for what I'm paying this guy, he'll dig all the way to China if he has to."

"Lordy, Sue Ann," the second woman said with a nervous laugh, "I'm glad you're not after *my* boyfriend."

"What makes you so sure she isn't?" the first woman asked.

Giggling like schoolgirls, the women climbed the porch steps and entered the house without spotting Rachel in the shadows.

Rachel found herself shaking harder than ever. She had to find out about her past before Sue Ann did. And once she knew the facts, she'd have to tell Wade.

Her heart sank like a stone in a pond. If she was married and had lied to him in her letters, he'd have to withdraw his proposal. Not that she'd blame him. She'd do the same in his place.

"Rachel, you all right?"

As if her thoughts had conjured him up, Wade stood beside her in the darkness.

"I'm...fine."

"You're sure? You disappeared so fast, I was afraid you might be ill."

She pushed out of her chair, crossed to the railing and gazed back toward the barn. "I'm fine. Just a little overwhelmed by all the excitement."

With the shadows etching his face, he looked even more attractive than she remembered.

Handsome, strong, dependable.

She wanted more than anything to throw herself in his arms and tell him everything. Except she didn't know the details of what might be a very sordid story.

"You're shivering." Wade stepped behind her and wrapped his arms around her. "Where's that sweater you had earlier?"

The warmth of his arms, the solidness of his body, the tenderness in his voice made her want to weep.

"I must have left it in the truck," she managed to answer between chattering teeth.

He threw his arm around her bare shoulders and pulled her toward the stairs. "Then we'll have to go get it. I—"

"Well, well, what have we here?" Sue Ann stepped out of the house. "You two been necking on my front porch like a couple of horny teenagers?"

"For Pete's sake, Sue Ann," Wade said in exasperation, "watch your mouth."

The woman's eyes glowed cold beneath the porch light. "Looks like you're the one should be watching your mouth and where you put it. Never know what you might catch from strange women."

Rachel felt Wade's muscles tighten.

"Dammit, Sue Ann," he said between gritted teeth, "that's enough. If you weren't a woman, I'd—"

"Oh, but I am a woman," Sue Ann purred. "Glad you finally noticed."

"See?" Throwing his hands wide in frustration, he turned to Rachel. "Talking to her is like talking to a post. She doesn't hear a word I say. Let's find your sweater before I forget she's a woman and pop her jaw.''

Taking Rachel by the elbow, he led her toward the lane where he'd parked the pickup. She had to take three steps to his one to keep up with him.

''Maybe we should leave,'' Rachel said.

Wade halted and stared down at her. ''I can be stubborn, too. I came to dance, and I won't let Sue Ann's bad manners drive me away.''

''You said you weren't a dancing man.''

The moonlight illuminated his grin. ''I told Sue Ann I wasn't a dancing man. But with you, Rachel, I intend to dance all night. Now let's get that sweater and hurry back to the barn.''

Rachel hung back. For a few minutes, she'd forgotten her memories of Ray and her in-laws. Now the reality of her fuzzy past crashed in on her again.

''What's wrong?'' Wade asked. ''You're not going to let a mean-spirited bitch like Sue Ann spoil your fun, are you?''

Taking a deep breath, she threw him a brave smile. ''No. I've never been fond of bullies.''

And Ray had been the biggest bully of them all. She thrust away the unwanted thought.

''Atta girl.''

Wade reached into the truck for her sweater and settled it around her. His hands lingered on her shoulders, and she fought the urge to turn into the comforting circle of his arms. She didn't deserve Wade. She'd violated his trust by her omissions of her past, and she couldn't even begin to set things right until she either remembered everything or dug up the facts for herself.

With his arm still draped around her, Wade nudged her gently toward the barn, and she fell into step beside him.

"Look," he said, "you've had a rough time the last few weeks. How about tonight you forget about the future and making decisions and just enjoy yourself?"

"I'll try." But she didn't sound convincing.

Heaven knew, she wanted to forget the past, the future, everything but the present, but focusing on the here and now wasn't as easy as Wade made it sound. Especially when she was enjoying the weight of his arm around her shoulders, the warmth of his body pressed against hers, and the caring in his voice. All that would end all too soon.

They reached the open double doors of the barn, and the easy strains of a slow tune filled the night air.

Wade smiled down at her with a leisurely, amiable look that made her grin back in spite of herself.

"Miss O'Riley," he said, opening his arms. "May I have this dance?"

Without having to think, she stepped into his embrace as easily as breathing.

JORDAN WATCHED HIS DAD lead Rachel onto the dance floor. The sight of them together gave him a warm, snuggly feeling deep inside. Rachel had fit into life at the ranch as easy as falling off a log, and she had made Jordan a whole lot happier and a lot less lonely.

He hoped Rachel was going to be his new mom. Nobody ever told him anything, but from the way his dad was looking at her, Jordan would bet next week's allowance that his dad liked her a lot.

Then he caught sight of Rachel's face. She looked as if her favorite dog had just died. When she saw Jordan watching her, she smiled and waved, but he could tell her heart wasn't in it.

He waved back and turned away, clenching his teeth with anger. If anybody had made Rachel unhappy, he'd guess it was Sue Ann Swenson. He'd seen the dirty looks his hostess had shot Rachel during supper. He glanced around the room in search of Sue Ann, and he wished he wasn't just a kid.

He didn't spot Sue Ann, but he caught the eye of Cindy Lou Sutton, a red-haired, freckled-faced girl from his class at school. Her face lit up like a moonstruck cow, and she started working her way across the dance floor toward him.

"Looks like you've found yourself a dancing partner," Ursula commented beside him.

"Not me. I'm not dancing with no girl."

Jordan rushed out of the barn and headed straight for the dessert table. He'd been so full right after supper, he hadn't had room for Ursula's five-layer chocolate cake, but he was hungry again now. He eyed the last wedge, placed it on a paper plate and scouted the area for a spot to enjoy the cake in peace. So far, Cindy Lou hadn't followed him out of the barn, but that didn't mean she wasn't still on his trail.

Skirting the huge building, he strolled to the back

of the barn. A huge pile of horse manure steamed in the moonlight, and he grinned when he saw it.

That would keep Cindy Lou away.

He perched on a stump someone had evidently used for splitting logs, and dug into his dessert. With the wind blowing the other way, he didn't mind the nearness of the manure pile at all. Nobody was going to bother him out here.

He'd just swallowed his first bite when someone tapped him on the shoulder, and he jumped like a frog on a hot griddle. He almost dropped his cake, but managed to fumble it to safety.

"What do mean, scaring a fellow to death like that?" he hollered.

Sue Ann Swenson towered above him. "I've been wanting to talk to you."

"What about?" Jordan eyed her warily and took another bite of cake.

"About your houseguest."

"Rachel?"

She grimaced at him. "You have another houseguest?"

"No, just Rachel."

"What do you think of her?"

"I like her."

"And your father?"

"He likes her, too." Jordan took another huge bite of cake and wished he'd brought a glass of milk along to wash it down.

Sue Ann folded her arms across her chest. "Does he ever kiss her?"

"Kissing? Yuck! My dad never kisses anybody."

"Not that you've seen."

Jordan thought about that for a minute. It was possible his dad kissed Rachel when he wasn't around, but he doubted it. Dancing tonight was the closest he'd ever seen the two together. "No, not that I've seen."

"Have you seen anything else?"

Jordan was fast losing interest in this conversation. He took another mouthful of cake.

"Pay attention when I'm talking to you." Sue Ann yanked the plate from his hand and tossed it on the manure pile behind her.

Jordan's anger swelled. He really liked Ursula's cake, and that had been the last piece.

"I don't know what you want me to say," he said with growing anger.

"I want you to tell me what a tramp Rachel is."

"Tramp?" Jordan didn't understand.

Sue Ann rolled her eyes toward the sky. "God spare me from innocents. Tramp, Jordan, like a loose woman who sneaks into your daddy's bed at night when everyone else is asleep."

Something inside Jordan snapped. He wasn't exactly sure what Sue Ann was driving at, but he knew from her tone it wasn't nice. With a growl, he leaped from the stump. "Just leave me alone."

She blocked his path. "I'm not finished."

"I am!" He pushed her out of his way.

With a shriek, Sue Ann flailed her arms and fell backward.

Directly into the pile of steaming manure.

Chapter Eleven

Wade found dancing with Rachel a bittersweet experience. She glanced up at him, laughing, obviously enjoying herself, and he was amazed to realize he was enjoying himself, too. For the first time in years. And when his arm brushed the curve of her breast, he smoldered with desire too long forgotten. He wanted this woman, wanted her in his life, in his bed, wanted to feel her body joined with his....

She fit into his arms as comfortably as if they'd been made for each other, two parts of a perfect whole. She was light on her feet, graceful as a butterfly.

And probably someone else's wife.

He silently cursed his rotten luck. The first woman to make him feel alive since Maggie's treachery, and he didn't even know her real name.

When the band ended their set, he was reluctant to let her go. She remained in his arms a beat after the music ended, as if she, too, was unwilling to break away.

Until a bloodcurdling scream broke the momentary silence, and they jumped apart.

"Stay here," Wade ordered, then sprinted outside toward the rear of the barn where the shriek had originated. Several other men followed close on his heels.

In the dim light, he could see a pair of white-clad legs kicking in the manure pile.

"Don't just stand there, you idiots," the woman yelled at them. "Pull me out of this mess!"

Nobody moved, and a few deep chuckles filled the odorous night air as the men recognized Sue Ann. Wade clamped his lips together to keep from laughing out loud.

He heard Leo behind him. "Miss Swenson, whatcha doing in that pile of horse sh—"

"Get me out of here, Wade Garrett," she bellowed, "so I can skin that son of yours alive. He pushed me!"

Wade sobered quickly at her accusation and glanced around to find Jordan nearby, eyes wide with apprehension.

"Is that true, son?" Wade asked. "Did you push her?"

Jordan cast his gaze toward his boots. "Yes, sir."

Jordan.

In trouble.

Again. Exasperation welled in Wade. "Why?"

"She was saying awful things—" With a glance over Wade's shoulder, Jordan broke off abruptly.

Wade turned to see Rachel standing behind him, her eyes glowing with curiosity, her lips twitching in a barely suppressed grin.

"It doesn't matter *what* Miss Swenson was saying,'' Wade admonished the boy. ''Nothing excuses what you did.''

Jordan hung his head again. ''No, sir.''

Rachel moved beside Jordan and placed an arm around his shoulders. She was hands down the prettiest, sexiest, most blood-stirring female Wade had ever met, and the desire he'd experienced while they danced resurrected itself.

The sight of her with her arm around his son in a protective maternal gesture temporarily cooled Wade's anger—until his memories of his father and his harsh discipline whispered in his head.

Before Wade could fault Rachel for coddling the boy, Sue Ann shrieked again, her scream splitting the night air and making the hair on the back of Wade's neck stand up. ''Isn't anyone going to help me up?''

Wade hurried to the steaming pile, plunged in up to his ankles and offered Sue Ann his hands.

Her body made a loud, sucking sound as he jerked her from the stinking heap of fresh dung. With muck matting her hair and dripping from her body, she resembled an alien blob from a class B horror movie.

''Pew-ee!'' Ken Johannson stepped forward to give Wade a hand. ''That shore is pungent perfume you're wearing tonight, Miss Swenson.''

Sue Ann gained her feet and stomped her boots, splattering manure all around her. The watching crowd scattered under the shower of muck. Catching sight of Jordan, she headed toward him with outstretched hands until Wade caught her and held her back. His hands slipped on the muck on her sleeves, and she almost managed to break free.

Wade tightened his grip.

"It's that little brat's fault," she yelled, kicking at Wade in an attempt to liberate herself. "Let me at him!"

"First thing you should do," Wade suggested calmly, "is go up to the house, change clothes and wash the muck out of your hair." He released her, placed himself between her and Jordan, and shot his son a stern glance. "Jordan's my responsibility."

"My clothes are ruined," Sue Ann whined.

"Send me a bill," Wade said. "Jordan, Rachel, we'll be heading home now."

Rachel steered Jordan toward the lane where the pickup was parked. Wade strode to the rear of the barn, cleaned his boots the best he could with fresh hay, and rinsed his hands under a spigot. Seething with frustration and anger, he stomped after Rachel and Jordan. The rest of the crowd had already returned to the dance, and Sue Ann had disappeared inside the ranch house. More than anything, he wanted off the Swenson ranch before he laid eyes on Sue Ann again. The woman was impossible.

Not that Jordan was any better.

His behavior had seemed to improve since Rachel arrived, but tonight, pushing his hostess into a mountain of stinking manure...

Uncontrollable laughter bubbled up from deep inside as he recalled Sue Ann's appearance when she emerged from the dung heap. He fought to control it before he reached the truck. The last thing Jordan needed was to think his father approved of what he'd done.

Wade swung into the cab of the truck, where Rachel and Jordan waited. No one spoke as he started the engine and headed toward home. He could have choked on the tension, but, afraid of saying the wrong thing, he said nothing.

When he pulled up in front of the house, Rachel and Jordan climbed out. In the moonlight, he could read clearly the look in her eyes, pleading with him to go easy on the boy.

But maybe that was Jordan's problem. In order to make up for the loss of his mother, maybe Wade had let him get away with too much. Jordan had to learn a lesson.

"Jordan," he called sharply. His son stopped his ascent of the front steps and turned slowly. "Yes, sir?"

"You're confined to your room for a week."

"Yes, sir."

The quiver in the boy's voice almost broke Wade's resolve. He could tell Jordan was exerting his utmost to keep from crying. "Ursula will bring your meals. And there'll be no video games or playing on the computer."

"Wade—" Rachel began, but he cut her off.

"Do you understand, Jordan?"

"Yes, sir. I'm sorry, Dad. I didn't mean for Miss Swenson to fall. I was just trying to get away."

Jordan looked so contrite, so small and miserable, that again Wade almost wavered. Then he remembered his own father's strong discipline and Maggie's penchant for breaking all the rules, and he hardened his heart.

"Go to bed, son. We'll talk tomorrow."

Rachel caught up with the boy, hugged him and kissed his cheek. Jordan clung to her for several seconds before breaking away and running inside.

Wade felt a pang of envy. He wanted Rachel to kiss him—but not that sweet, maternal peck. He wanted to feel her fire and passion, to taste her—

"Weren't you a bit harsh?" she asked when the front door closed behind Jordan, interrupting Wade's wishful thoughts.

He caught a whiff of himself, still sporting a layer of manure from his rescue of Sue Ann. Even if he felt free to kiss her, she'd probably as soon kiss a pig. As for her question, he was in no mood for discussion, and denying his inner yearnings did nothing to sweeten his temper. "The boy has to learn he can't go knocking people down."

"What if it really was an accident, like he said?" she demanded in a soft, gentle voice that played havoc with Wade's insides.

"It's his word against Sue Ann's."

"Yes, it is," she said bluntly. "*That* should make you think twice."

Rachel had a point. Sue Ann was famous for twisting the truth to suit her own needs.

"Maybe," she said, "you should learn to trust your son."

Frustration over Jordan and over Rachel's unknown identity consumed Wade like ants under his skin. Exhaustion made him surly. "I can't stand here arguing in the moonlight. I stink to high heaven—"

"And you're exhausted from a long day's work," she added reasonably. "You should get some rest."

She mounted the stairs and crossed the porch toward the front door. Somehow her sensible attitude only irritated him further.

"Rachel?"

"Yes?" She stepped to the edge of the porch, into a pool of moonlight that made her look as if she'd been dipped in silver, a shimmering goddess far beyond his reach.

He wanted her to stay forever, to help him with Jordan, but most of all, to help him with himself. He needed her kisses, her soft touches. He needed her in all the ways a man needed a woman, a very special woman. He'd developed too hard a skin, too many rough edges since Maggie died. He wanted to make love to Rachel until he couldn't draw breath.

To marry her.

Grow old with her.

And he didn't even know her real name.

She was watching him, her feathery eyebrows lifted, her green eyes questioning.

"Good night," he said, his voice almost breaking with emotion. "We'll talk in the morning."

"Good night, Wade." Her voice caressed him like a kiss, and he had to restrain himself from bounding up the steps after her and pulling her into his arms.

Only two things held him back.

Her unknown identity.

And an odorous coating of horse manure.

FOR THE FIRST TIME since Rachel had arrived at the ranch, Ursula wasn't in the big kitchen when Rachel went down for breakfast the next morning. She guessed the housekeeper must either be sleeping late after the night's festivities, attending church or battling a bout of arthritis.

Rachel made a pot of extra strong coffee to keep her awake. She hadn't slept well, afraid to drop into unconsciousness and dream about Ray and her previous life. What she had already remembered wasn't pretty, and she feared learning more. She was thankful now for Wade's suggestion that she delay accepting his proposal. Before she made any commitment, she had to know the facts of her identity.

But lying awake had proved as distressful as her unwanted dreams. She kept remembering the feel of Wade's arms around her at the dance, how warm, strong and solid he'd felt. All night her rebellious body had ached for him with a passion that had overwhelmed her, making sleep impossible, even if she'd wanted it. The only way to cut short her suffering was to find out the truth about herself.

She considered asking Sheriff Howard for help. After all, he had her mug shot and her fingerprints. But he was also Wade's best friend, and she wasn't sure she could trust the lawman not to tell Wade before she discovered what she needed to know. She needed to talk with Dr. Sinclair to make sure she wasn't hallucinating a former existence before she proceeded with her search.

Remembering Jordan confined to his room, she prepared breakfast for two on a tray, climbed the stairs to his room, and knocked lightly on his door.

He opened it almost immediately, and when he

saw her, his expression brightened. "I thought you were Ursula."

She was struck again by how much he resembled his father, which only increased her already sizable affection for the boy. "I brought our breakfast."

Anxiety glittered in his eyes. "Are you sure it's all right with Dad?"

Rachel stepped into the room and closed the door behind her with her hip. "He said you couldn't leave your room. I didn't hear him say anything about no one coming in."

She set the tray on Jordan's desk and glanced around. For a small boy, he kept his room unusually immaculate. It contained the usual boy paraphernalia—bird nests, action figures, model planes and his budding rock collection—but everything was arranged with neatness and precision. His freshly made bed would have passed military inspection.

"This is a great room." She nodded toward the windows, where a pair of binoculars sat on the sill. "And you have a terrific view of the barn and the mountains behind it."

"I like to watch for birds. And at night I use a telescope to identify the constellations."

Her heart went out to him. Obviously the boy spent a lot of his time alone. At least he'd learned to entertain himself.

"What's that yummy smell?" Jordan gazed hungrily at the tray Rachel had covered with a clean dishcloth.

"Oatmeal."

"Oatmeal! Major yuck!"

She flashed him a smile. "Why, Jordan Garrett,

how can you say that when you've never tried *my* oatmeal?''

''Probably the same old lumpy mess Ursula tries to feed me.''

Rachel whisked the cloth off the tray. ''Does Ursula put cinnamon and brown sugar in hers?''

The delectable aroma wafted across the room, and Jordan sniffed appreciatively. ''I don't think so.''

''And raisins and walnuts?''

''Uh-uh.''

''Tell you what,'' Rachel bargained, ''try one bite. If you don't like it, I'll take it back downstairs and scramble you some eggs.''

He took the bowl and spoon she handed him and warily tried a mouthful. His lips lifted in a grin. ''Wow, this is super.''

''And there's orange juice, milk and some of Ursula's sticky buns.''

''Gosh, Rachel,'' Jordan said between bites. ''This is fun. I wish you could fix my breakfast all the time.''

With her own bowl of oatmeal, Rachel perched on the side of the bed. She, too, wished she could stay. To fix Jordan's breakfast after a night spent with Wade...

''I'll make you a deal. As long as you're under lock and key, I'll bring your breakfast. How's that?''

''Awesome.'' His expression sobered. ''As long as Dad doesn't mind.''

''How can he mind? You have to eat.''

''You don't know my dad. He always minds about something.''

Rachel thought of Wade and his ongoing frustration over raising Jordan alone. "You're lucky your father loves you enough to keep you on the right track."

"I guess," Jordan said with a sigh. "I just wish I didn't make him mad at me so much."

Rachel didn't know what to say. She wished she could tell Jordan she'd stay at the ranch and help him understand his father better. She wished she could stay to assuage the loneliness she glimpsed so often in Wade's eyes, but she had no idea what her future held. Not until she figured out her past.

"Rachel?"

"Hmm?" She raised her eyes from her coffee cup to find Jordan staring at her.

"You're cool, Rachel. I wish you were my mom."

"I wish that, too, Jordan. I'd give my right arm for a son like you." Tears welled unexpectedly in her eyes, and she forced a smile. "Now, eat up. There're sticky buns left."

WADE PACED THE KITCHEN floor, waiting for Rachel to appear. He hadn't slept well. All night, the memory of Rachel in his arms, imprinted indelibly on his muscles, had made him ache with desire. He'd lain awake and cursed himself for falling in love with a woman he couldn't have. And he'd risen this morning with a headache worse than a hangover after a four-day binge.

Someone had made coffee, and he'd almost finished the pot. The extra jolt of caffeine hadn't been such a good idea, not with his nerves already jangling over the prospect of revealing Maggie's story, but at least he was wide awake. Now that he'd promised to tell Rachel about his deceased wife, he wanted to get it over with.

He'd about decided to rush upstairs and bang on her door to awaken her when she breezed into the kitchen, carrying a tray of dirty dishes.

"Where've you been?" he blurted, his gruffness covering the surge of tenderness he experienced at her arrival. She looked even prettier than usual this morning, her cheeks glowing, her hair shining in the morning sun and her snug jeans tempting him with curves he dare not touch.

"Good morning to you, too," she said with a sweetness he should have been accustomed to, but which still managed to take his breath away.

"Good morning." Chastised, he took the heavy tray from her and set it next to the sink. "Did you have breakfast in your room?"

She crossed to the sink and began filling it with hot water. "I had breakfast with Jordan."

"With Jordan?"

"The child has to eat."

"He should eat alone. He's being punished."

"Yes, he is," she said with a wry smile that managed to creep under his skin. "For something that probably wasn't even his fault."

"We went around and around on that last night. Don't start again."

She plunged the dirty dishes into soapy water. "You're the boss."

"Leave those." He placed his hand on her shoulder, then jerked it away as if burned. He couldn't risk touching her. Once he started, he didn't know if he could stop. "I want to talk to you."

"I'm listening."

"Not here." Wade glanced upward toward his son's room. "I can't risk Jordan overhearing." He shifted impatiently from foot to foot while she dried her hands. "Come with me."

Rachel followed him through the house and out the front door. He pointed to a path that led through the trees to the river. Side by side, they plunged into the deep shade of the overgrown trail.

The morning sun had already burned away the mist, and the day promised to be warm. Wade welcomed the coolness beneath the trees as he held branches aside for Rachel to pass. He was all too conscious of her presence—the gracefulness of her gliding walk; the way she quickened her steps to match his stride; her unique fragrance, a blend of soap, sweetness, and femininity—and he wished the purpose of their walk was a romantic rendezvous away from the dozens of prying eyes at the ranch.

Instead, he would be sharing the most painful, humiliating episode of his life.

All too soon he could hear the river, flooded with melting snow from the high country, bounding over its rocky bed. They rounded a bend in the path that brought them to the riverbank.

"It's beautiful here." Rachel glanced at the sunlight filtering through the trees and creating explosions of light on the rapids below. "Like an outdoor cathedral."

At the river's edge, Wade gestured toward a rustic

bench made of split logs. "I used to spend a lot of time here when I was a kid."

Rachel settled on the log seat. "Why not now?"

Wade sat beside her, his gaze on the river. He didn't dare look at her, or he'd grab her and kiss her senseless. "Running the ranch takes all my time."

"Seems a shame to live near such beauty and not take advantage of it."

He dived head on into the subject he'd come there to discuss. Its unpleasantness cooled his ardor. "I used to bring Maggie here when we were dating."

He turned to find Rachel studying him with cool green eyes. "Are you sure that's not the reason you've avoided this spot until now?" she asked.

Her perception racheted his frustration up another notch. The one woman he'd ever met who appeared to understand him as easily as breathing was beyond his reach.

He plunged into his story before he lost his nerve. "Maggie was eighteen when we married. I'd always thought of her as just a kid—she was six years younger than me—until I saw her at one of the Swenson barn dances. Overnight she'd turned into a beautiful, vivacious girl. Dark wavy hair, flashing eyes and a come-on smile. Every guy in the county was crazy about her. I don't know why she picked me."

"She obviously knew quality when she saw it," Rachel said with a warm smile that made him want to sit on his hands to keep from reaching for her.

"We were happy at first," he continued, "but she became pregnant with Jordan almost immediately, and she hated losing her figure. She hated everything about being pregnant.''

''She was still just a girl.''

Wade nodded, and with stunning clarity, realized Maggie had never matured. She'd always been a young girl, aching for parties, fun and adventure. She hadn't lived long enough to develop into a woman.

Certainly not the kind of woman Rachel was— calm, assured, comfortable with herself.

''He was born the day before her nineteenth birthday. Although she seemed to adore him, she turned Jordan over to Ursula's care as soon as she brought him home from the hospital. That's when the real trouble began.''

Rachel sat motionless, listening with a gravity that eased his embarrassment at the telling.

''After Jordan was born, Maggie was never home. She kept later and later hours, and sometimes disappeared overnight. She always had a reasonable explanation—helping her mother, visiting a sick friend, driving all the way to Kalispell to take in a movie.''

He picked up a rock from the riverbank and pitched it into the swirling water. ''But all her excuses were lies.''

Rachel reached over and placed her hand on his. Her skin was soft and warm, and he knew he should pull away, but he reveled in her nearness. Too soon she would be gone.

''I'm sorry,'' she said.

Years of bitterness eased with her touch, and he realized with a jolt that this healing had begun the day Rachel had entered his life. For the first time, he was able to look back at Maggie objectively. His wife hadn't been a bad person, just a girl who married and became a mother too young, who hadn't had a chance to stretch her wings before she settled down. He felt as if a block of ice around his heart had been melting away since Rachel arrived, and the corrosive jealousy and resentment that had haunted him for so long had miraculously disappeared.

He had Rachel to thank for washing away his bitterness, and he longed to gather her in his arms, but he had to finish his story—the worst part.

"After Jordan's birth, the doctors warned Maggie against having more children because she'd had such a difficult time with the delivery, but Maggie never listened to what anyone told her. Jordan was still a toddler when Maggie became pregnant again."

Wade dragged his fingers through his hair and forced out words he'd never told anyone else. "The baby wasn't mine. Maggie and I hadn't made love in over a year when she became pregnant. She never told me who the father was."

"That must have been an awful time for you," Rachel said quietly.

Wade nodded. "For Jordan's sake, I begged Maggie to stay with us. Promised her I'd raise the child as if it were my own. She agreed to try to make our marriage work again, but it was too late."

He shoved himself to his feet and paced over the rocky bank. "She and the baby died."

Rachel rose and looped her arm through his. "Poor Maggie."

"Yeah." Tears welled in Wade's eyes and a knot formed in his throat. He was finally able to mourn Maggie without animosity and the desire for retribution. "Poor Maggie."

"It must have been hard for you. Widowed with a young child."

Wade scuffed a rock with the toe of his boot. "I'm ashamed to admit it now, but what was worst for me was my wounded pride. I felt like every person in Lincoln County knew Maggie had made a fool of me, and I hated her for it. Her own family moved away to avoid the shame."

"Is that why you've never talked to Jordan about his mother?"

"I'm not proud of that, but what could I tell him? That his mother was a liar and a tramp?"

Rachel shook her head. "Tell him what he needs to know."

Wade looked at her, not understanding.

"Tell him," Rachel said, "that his mother was a lovely, vivacious woman who loved him and you in her own way."

He placed his hands on her shoulders and met her calm gaze. "Where did you learn to be so wise?"

"You know I can't answer that," she said with a self-effacing smile.

Without his noticing it, Rachel had gradually healed his aching heart and his wounded pride. More than anything, he wanted to thank her by holding her in his arms and kissing those soft, coral lips. He leaned toward her and felt the warmth of her breath against his lips.

Alarm flashed in her green eyes, and she jerked away.

What had frightened her? he wondered, then realized her withdrawal was best for both of them. He had told her Maggie's story to buy himself time until her identity was discovered. If he kissed her again, he'd want more than a kiss. He wanted to make love to Rachel, to sample her sweetness and give her pleasure. He wanted to watch her respond to his caresses. But he had no right to take what he wanted, not when she might belong to another man. If he kissed her again, he'd ruin everything.

"Maybe we should go back to the house," she suggested in a breathless voice.

They both turned from the river at the sound of someone crashing through the undergrowth behind them.

"Wade, where are you?" Leo's voice boomed out from the path.

Wade greeted his foreman as Leo strode into sight. "What are you doing out here on a Sunday morning?"

"I have to talk to you about Jordan," Leo said.

"Good grief," Wade said in exasperation. "What's the boy done now?"

Before Leo could answer, the sound of a wildly tolling bell filled the air.

"What's that?" Rachel asked.

"There's an emergency at the ranch." Wade broke into a run, with Leo fast on his heels. "Hurry!"

Chapter Twelve

Wade raced toward the house, his heart beating as hard as his boots pounded the pathway. Everyone on the ranch had strict instructions *never* to ring the bell by the front drive except in the direst emergency, a crisis like injury, fire, severe weather.

The mournful sound of that bell filled him with fear. The last time it had rung, his father had suffered a fatal heart attack in the barn. Wade couldn't imagine, didn't want to guess what catastrophe had struck now.

He broke through the bushes into the yard to find Jordan swinging on the end of the cord, yanking the bell with all his skinny might.

Wade exploded with rage. "What the hell do you think you're doing? You're supposed to be in your room!"

Jordan pointed toward the barn. "But, Dad—"

"No back talk, young man—"

Wade's gaze followed Jordan's gesture, and his heart leaped to his throat. In the woods behind the barn, flames were crowning in the tops of the trees.

A strong wind was pushing the fire directly toward the ranch buildings.

"It's a sleeper from the lightning storm," Jordan said. "I saw the smoke from my bedroom window."

At the tolling of the bell, ranch hands, accustomed to sleeping in on Sunday mornings, poured from the bunkhouse, jerking on boots and jackets as they came.

Behind Wade, Lefty Starr sprinted up the drive from the front gate, rifle in hand.

"Leo," Wade ordered as the foreman joined him, "have the hands evacuate the horses into the east pasture. I'll use the tractor to plow a firebreak behind the barn."

"What about me, Dad?" Jordan asked. "What can I do?"

"Me, too," Rachel said, out of breath from her trek from the river.

"Get feed sacks from the barn," Wade said, "and wet them down. You'll need to watch for sparks blowing into the grass, and beat them out."

Wade rushed to the barn with his workers behind him. While the hands led the horses from their stalls, Leo helped Wade attach the harrow to the tractor.

"Damn wind's pushing the fire fast," the old foreman said. "You'll have to hurry."

Wade started the tractor and drove it out the barn's rear doors. Thick smoke choked him, and he stopped long enough to wet a bandanna and tie it over his nose and mouth, then he hopped onto the tractor again. If he could strip the earth of grass between the woods and the clearing behind the barn, the fire would die for lack of fuel.

Through the thickening smoke, he could see the hands leading the terrified horses out of the barn. Behind the barn, Rachel, Jordan and Ursula, the lower half of their faces covered with wet kerchiefs against the smoke, attacked hot spots in the grass with wet burlap sacks.

The heat from the fire seared his skin, and sweat poured into his eyes, but he continued driving through the suffocating smoke, turning the dried grass under with the plow blade.

For what seemed hours, he drove back and forth, widening the firebreak, until his lungs felt as if they would burst from smoke and his skin felt blistered from the heat. But he couldn't quit. If the fire reached the barn, the wind would blow it toward the house, and he wasn't going to lose the Garrett homestead to a damned lightning strike. Not while there was still breath in his body.

Suddenly he realized he wasn't alone. A large Forest Service earth mover appeared beside him, gouging huge swaths between the fire and the barn, increasing the distance the fire would have to leap to reach the buildings.

Above the roar of the vehicles, Wade could hear the ranger issuing orders to his smokechasers. Then came the rumble of another engine as a Forest Service tanker crew arrived and began to spray the fast-approaching blaze with water.

Someone on the fire line cheered. Wade lifted his head and realized the wind had shifted, blowing the fire back over woods it had already consumed. It was out of fuel.

The worst was over.

For another hour, Wade and his hands battled hot spots in the woods with the Forest Service crew until the fire no longer threatened to flare up and damage any ranch buildings. Aching, soot covered, his throat raw and his eyes watering from smoke, he finally walked back toward the barn.

Ursula and Jordan were pouring cold drinks for the firefighters, and Wade gratefully accepted a glass of iced tea.

"Is it out for good?" Jordan asked.

Wade looked at his son with a lump in his throat. If it hadn't been for Jordan's sharp eyes, they might have lost the barn and outbuildings, the horses and the main house.

"Thank you, son. Without your early warning, this could have been a real disaster."

"Three cheers for Jordan," Leo cried, and the hands and other firefighters joined in the praise and applause.

Jordan blushed with pleasure, but his expression quickly sobered. He gazed at his father with solemn eyes. "If you don't need me, sir, I'd better return to my room."

Without a backward look, the boy trudged toward the ranch house.

"I need to talk to you about that boy," Leo said.

Wade poured himself another glass of tea and settled on a bench. "I'm listening."

"I was out behind the Swenson barn last night," Leo said, "having myself a smoke. You know how Ursula is about my cigarettes."

Wade nodded.

"Anyways," the foreman continued, "I saw the

whole exchange between Sue Ann and Jordan. She was making insinuations about you and Miss Rachel.''

''What kind of insinuations?''

''They was pretty crude and don't bear repeating. The boy asked her to stop, but she wouldn't. When he tried to get away from her, she blocked his way. He was just trying to get around her when she fell in the muck. It wasn't the boy's fault.''

Wade sighed. Rachel had told him so. He should have listened to her.

Rachel.

''Where's Rachel?'' he asked.

Leo shrugged. ''Last time I saw her, she was with Jordan.''

Wade searched for Rachel among the crowd of firefighters but didn't see her. He handed Leo his empty glass and raced after Jordan, catching up with the boy at the front steps.

''Jordan,'' he called.

The boy turned and cringed when he saw his father. ''I'm going straight back to my room. Honest, Dad.''

With a twinge of guilt at his son's fear of him, Wade pulled Jordan into his arms. ''Your punishment's been lifted. Leo saw what happened last night and backs up your side of the story.''

The boy's face brightened. ''Really?''

''Now,'' Wade said, ''where's Rachel? Inside?''

Jordan shook his head and pointed to the river path. ''She went that way. And he went with her.''

''He?'' Wade felt a terrible sense of foreboding.

"That Mr. Crutchfield, the insurance adjustor guy."

"Go find Lefty and Leo," Wade ordered. "Tell them to bring their guns and meet me at the river."

With his heart again pounding in his throat, he set off at a dead run down the path.

EXHAUSTED, RACHEL slumped on the porch steps. Her back ached and her hands were rubbed raw from handling the wet burlap. The fire was practically out, the barn was saved and no one had been hurt, thanks to Jordan's early warning. Wade and the others were still mopping up the remnants of the blaze.

Jordan sprawled on the stairs beside her, drinking cola from a can, looking like a raccoon with his face begrimed with soot.

"Your sharp eyes and quick action saved the barn," she said. "Your dad must be really proud of you."

"I don't know," Jordan said with a doubtful shake of his head. "After last night, he thinks I'm a juvenile delinquent."

"No, he doesn't."

"Then why did he lock me up like a criminal?"

Rachel didn't have an answer. After hearing Wade tell Maggie's story, she better understood his adherence to strict discipline. She also understood how much he needed a woman who loved him, and how much Jordan needed a mother. Both were responsibilities she'd love to assume, but not until she'd uncovered her past. She knew she should drive into Libby to talk with Dr. Sinclair, but she was too tired to move.

"Who's that?" Jordan pointed to a man walking up the drive from the main road.

Rachel squinted at the familiar figure. "It's Mr. Crutchfield, the insurance adjustor. Your dad must have called him."

When Crutchfield spotted her, he hurried toward the house.

"You here about the fire?" she asked as he approached.

The man glanced nervously from side to side. "Miss, um, O'Riley." He hesitated and nodded toward Jordan. "I must speak with you in private."

Rachel paused for a moment, gauging the wisdom of being alone with a stranger, but decided she was safe enough with Wade, Leo and so many others only a shout away. "Jordan, go see if Ursula needs some help."

With a final curious look at the newcomer, Jordan rose from the steps and jogged across the lawn toward the barn.

"What did you want to talk to me about, Mr. Crutchfield?"

"Is there some place private we can go?"

"What's wrong with here?"

Shifting uneasily from one foot to the other, the man kept glancing toward the barn. "I have information about your past, information Mr. Garrett doesn't want you to know. He's ordered me off the ranch before, and if he finds me here, he'll throw me out again."

Rachel shook her head. "That's ridicu…"

She remembered Lefty posted at the gate with a gun for reasons no one seemed inclined to explain to her. Right now, more than anything, she wanted to learn more about her life before the accident. If Crutchfield could help her...

"Come with me. There's a secluded spot by the river. No one can see us there."

Her pulse racing with excitement, she hurried down the trail with Crutchfield behind her. When she reached the rustic bench, she turned to him. "What do you know about my past?"

His eyes turned hard and cold. "I know you're *not* Rachel O'Riley."

Her first reaction was disbelief. "How would you know?"

"Because Rachel O'Riley worked for me in Atlanta, and I was going to marry her."

Sudden dizziness assailed her, and Rachel sank onto the bench. "Does Wade know I'm not Rachel?"

Crutchfield nodded grimly. "He's known since my first visit. He doesn't want you to find out."

A thousand questions plagued her, but one predominated. "If I'm not Rachel O'Riley, who *am* I?"

Crutchfield sat beside her and leaned closer with a menacing stare. "That is what I'm here to find out."

Why hadn't Wade told her? Did he know her real identity? And where was the Rachel O'Riley who had agreed to Wade's proposal?

Crutchfield grabbed her by the shoulders, and his fingers bit painfully into her skin. "Tell me your real name."

Fear mixed with her bewilderment. "I can't. I don't remember."

He shook her forcefully. "Think! You have to remember. I need your name."

She tried to push him away, but the man was too strong. "I don't *know* my name."

"Let her go, Crutchfield." Wade's commanding voice echoed along the riverbank.

Crutchfield released her and sprang away from the bench. "You can't keep her here forever under false pretenses, Garrett. There're laws—"

"And there're laws against trespassing, too." Wade cocked his rifle with an ominous snap that made Crutchfield cringe.

Rachel had never been so glad to see anyone in her life as she was to see Wade. Her fear melted away, but her confusion remained.

Behind Wade stood Lefty, armed with his own rifle, and Leo with a shotgun.

"Leo," Wade said, "take our *visitor* up to the house and call Dan Howard. We'll let the sheriff take care of him."

Leo and Lefty led Crutchfield away but not before the trespasser shot Rachel a look of pure venom.

"Are you okay?" Wade asked.

Rachel vacillated between wanting to hug Wade for rescuing her, and smacking him for not telling her about herself.

"Is it true?" she demanded.

Wade leaned the rifle against the bench and sat down. "Is what true? Sounded like Crutchfield was shooting off his mouth about a lot of things."

"Am I Rachel O'Riley?"

"No." Grime and exhaustion etched his face,

making his expression impossible to read, especially since he refused to meet her gaze.

She struggled with a conflux of emotions, anger the foremost. "Why didn't you tell me?"

"Dr. Sinclair warned me not to, not until your memories returned."

She pivoted quickly on her heel and started up the path toward the house.

Wade sprang from the bench and grabbed her wrist. "Where are you going?"

"Home."

He raked the fingers of his other hand through smoke-streaked hair. "Rachel—"

"I'm *not* Rachel."

"You can't go home. You don't know where it is."

She wrenched from his grip. "Then it's about time I found out."

Without a backward look, she fled toward the ranch. The undergrowth along the path lashed her face, and she welcomed the sting that momentarily distracted her from the pain in her heart, the confusion in her mind.

Who was she?

Her mind remained a blank, registering pain and confusion, but no answers to her question. She slowed when she reached the front of the house and saw the pickup pull away, with Crutchfield sandwiched between Lefty and Leo in the front seat. Thankful no one else was around, she ran up the porch steps and into the house.

Fighting to hold back tears, she sprinted up the stairs to her room. She didn't have luggage, so she spread her jacket on the bed to use as a makeshift carryall, and began piling her clothes on top of it.

At least her crazy dreams made some sense now. If she wasn't Rachel, she must be the Jennifer from her dreams. The realization stopped her cold.

She was married.

To a man she no longer loved.

And she'd fallen hopelessly in love with Wade Garrett. With his son. With his home. With everything about him. Only she wasn't free to love anyone else. And she wasn't the woman he'd proposed to.

"Rachel, what are you doing?" Jordan stood in the doorway.

"Packing."

"Why?"

"I'm going away."

"You're leaving us?"

The hurt in the boy's voice wounded her, adding another fissure to her already breaking heart.

"I have to go, Jordan." She kept her gaze on her packing, but she could hear the tears in his voice.

"It's my fault, isn't it? You're leaving because I'm always in trouble."

She turned at his anguished cry and rushed to him. Going down on her knees, she pulled him close in a fierce bear hug. "You're a terrific kid, Jordan, and I love you."

"Then why do you have to go?" he sobbed into her neck, his tears wetting the collar of her shirt.

"It's complicated." She rubbed his back in a soothing gesture. "Your father will tell you."

"No, he won't." Jordan jerked away. "Dad never tells me anything."

She sat on the floor, leaned against the bed and pulled Jordan beside her, wrapping her arm around him. "I'll try to explain."

She recounted what she'd been told of the train wreck and her being identified as Rachel. "The hospital contacted your father because he was expecting Rachel O'Riley for a visit." She omitted the part about Wade's marriage proposal. "That's when he invited me here."

"Yeah, I know all that." Jordan's sobs had ended. "But I still don't know why you have to go."

"Remember when Mr. Crutchfield came to talk to me today?"

Jordan nodded.

"He knows Rachel O'Riley, and he says that's not who I am."

"Gosh, if you're not Rachel, who are you?"

She hugged the boy closer. "I don't know. That's why I have to leave, to learn who I am."

Jordan relaxed against her. "I get it. And you'll come back as soon as you find out?"

A sob caught in her throat, and she swallowed hard to keep from crying. "I may have a family of my own somewhere, waiting for me to come home."

She glanced up to find Wade standing in the doorway. He had showered and changed clothes, and he looked more handsome than she'd ever seen him.

"Jordan," he said. "I need to talk to Rachel alone."

The boy clambered to his feet. "You won't leave," he asked, "without saying goodbye?"

She shook her head. "I promise."

Jordan scurried from the room.

Wade reached down beside the door, lifted a suitcase and placed it on her bed. "You'll be needing this."

He was keeping his emotions under tight wraps, and she couldn't decipher his feelings.

"Sheriff Howard just called," he said. "He's discovered your real name."

She froze where she stood, knowing what was coming.

"You're Jennifer Reid," Wade said. "*Mrs*. Jennifer Reid."

Chapter Thirteen

Wade watched her face for a reaction, but she looked mostly dazed. He'd been stunned himself when he'd spoken with Dan Howard earlier.

"Someone filed a missing person report on her," the sheriff had said. "The report contains pictures. Jennifer Reid's your girl all right."

Wade had grabbed a pencil and scribbled the address Dan gave him. "Have Lefty and Leo arrived with Crutchfield? We caught him trespassing here earlier."

"They haven't come in yet, but you know I can't charge him for trespassing, not unless I or a deputy caught him in the act. I'll have to let him go."

"Will you tell him about Jennifer Reid?"

Dan snorted a laugh. "I figure this is a need-to-know situation. If the real Rachel O'Riley is trying to get away from him, then he doesn't need to know what name she might be using."

Returning to his current dilemma, Wade looked at the woman who had sunk onto the edge of the bed at his news. "Should I call you Jennifer?"

She glanced up with a pinched smile. "You've always called me Rachel. That's easier."

Wade nodded. "Well, I'd better go pack."

She looked surprised. "Why?"

"I'm taking you home."

"Home?"

"Memphis, Tennessee. We fly out tonight."

"I don't understand."

At the sight of the adorable wrinkle in her forehead, he felt his heart had been kicked by a wild mustang. "Understand what?"

"Why you're going with me."

He wasn't sure he understood completely himself. "I got you into this. Looks like it's up to me to get you out."

RACHEL—she still couldn't think of herself as Jennifer—unfastened her seat belt and gazed out the window. Below, stretched out like a topographic map, lay the Rocky Mountains of Montana, silhouetted by the setting sun. She experienced a spasm of regret at leaving the Big Sky Country as the plane climbed above the clouds, obscuring the view. She had come to love Montana. It felt like home.

But home was a suburb of Memphis, a place she couldn't remember, a place she dreaded, from what she'd seen in her dreams.

She glanced at Wade in the seat beside her. "Did Sheriff Howard tell you anything else about me?"

"Only that your attorney will meet us at the airport with the keys to your house."

"An attorney and not my family? That's odd." The news sent a cold chill down her spine. Her hus-

band must not be very anxious to see her. Not that
she was looking forward to a reunion with him, if
her dreams had been accurate.

"You're shivering," Wade said. "Are you
cold?"

"Yes," she lied, ashamed of her fears.

He signaled to the flight attendant, who brought
a blanket and pillow. With a tenderness that made
her want to weep, he settled the pillow behind her
head and tucked the blanket around her.

"Get some sleep," he said with a huskiness in
his voice she'd never heard before. "You've had a
rough day."

"I can't sleep. Too many unanswered questions
buzzing in my head."

"Dr. Sinclair wants you to be rested when you
arrive. She's hoping familiar surroundings will jar
your memories loose."

Obediently, Rachel closed her eyes, but the questions persisted. Where was her husband, and why
wasn't he meeting her, instead of an attorney? Why
had she left him? Where had she been headed when
the train was wrecked in Montana? What had happened to the rest of her family? Did she have children?

In spite of her uncertainties, she dropped off to
sleep, not to awaken until the pilot's voice on the
public address system announced their descent to the
Memphis airport.

Leaving the plane, she was grateful for Wade's
rock-steady presence, for her knees threatened to
buckle from a bad case of nerves.

"Chin up," he told her with an encouraging smile. "Everything's going to be fine."

But she knew nothing was going to be fine again, not when she wanted more than anything to return to the plane and fly with Wade back to Montana and Jordan. A chilling thought hit her. Wade was being so pleasant and helpful. Was he sorry to see her go or glad to be rid of her?

"Mrs. Reid?" A tall, slim man with white hair, a pencil-thin mustache and a welcoming smile was waiting at airside. "Jennifer?"

She took several seconds to realize he was speaking to her. She still thought of herself as Rachel. Still *wished* she was Rachel. "Yes?"

His smile dissolved. "You don't remember me? I'm Harold Lacy, your attorney, and your father's attorney before you."

Wade squeezed her arm reassuringly. "She doesn't remember anyone, Mr. Lacy. I'm Wade Garrett. We spoke on the phone earlier today. Mrs. Reid has been our guest since the accident."

She glanced behind the older man. "Are any of my family here?"

A dismayed look flashed across his face before he composed his features. "No, um, I'm alone tonight. We'll talk about the others in the morning."

She couldn't help noting the scowl on Wade's face, a clear indication that he wasn't happy with her lack of welcome.

"It's very late," Lacy said, "and I'm sure you'll want to go directly home."

She didn't know what to say, couldn't understand the implications of her family's abandonment, and she ached with exhaustion in spite of her nap on the plane.

Luckily, Wade wasn't struck mute as she'd been. "If you have the keys and directions to Mrs. Reid's house—"

"They're here." Lacy handed over a packet. "And the keys to your rental car."

"Mr. Lacy," Rachel asked, "will there be anyone waiting at home for me?"

He took her hands and gazed at her with sadness and compassion. "No, Jennifer. There's no one there except Marie, the housekeeper. I had her open the house when I knew you were arriving. I'll come around first thing tomorrow morning and explain everything. Good night."

The attorney left, and Wade hurried her forward to pick up their car. After a few instructions from the clerk at the desk, and with the use of Lacy's map, he drove through the streets of Memphis. When he reached the turnoff Lacy had marked, he whistled in surprise. "This is some fancy neighborhood, Mrs. Reid."

Rachel flinched at the strange name and gazed out the window. In spite of the darkness, the entrance to the gated community was well lit. When Wade gave her name to the security guard, he waved them through. She watched with detached interest as they drove past grand, expensive houses, set well back from the street, but nothing seemed familiar.

After a couple blocks, Wade turned the car into a drive blocked by an iron gate. He pulled up to a keypad set in a brick column, punched in a code, and the gate swung wide.

He placed his hand over hers. "Recognize anything?"

She shook her head, unable to speak without her voice quivering with anxiety.

He drove up a curved drive beneath an arch of magnolia trees and stopped beneath a columned portico. The heavy oak door opened wide, and a tiny, middle-aged woman stood on the threshold.

"Welcome home, Mrs. Reid. Hello, Mr. Garrett. I'll take your bags."

"Not necessary." Wade hopped from the car and picked up her single piece of luggage. "Just tell me where to put this."

"The first room on the right at the top of the stairs," Marie instructed. "And your room, Mr. Garrett, is three doors farther down on the left."

Wade shook his head. "I'm going to a motel as soon as I get Mrs. Reid settled."

"No," Rachel begged as she climbed out of the car. She knew they'd have to part, but she couldn't stand having to separate so soon. "Please stay. I'd like to see at least one familiar face in the morning."

"It's no trouble," Marie said. "We were expecting you to stay."

"We?" Rachel asked in alarm.

"Mr. Lacy and I," Marie said. "He made all the arrangements."

They followed the maid into the foyer, a high-ceilinged room with marble floors and a massive chandelier. Rachel found the space cold and forbidding.

Wade started up a curving marble staircase with a banister of carved mahogany. Rachel followed, and their footsteps echoed in the cavernous space of the enormous house.

On the second floor, Wade opened the first door on the right and placed her luggage on the bed. "Get some rest. You're all worn out. I'll see you in the morning."

Rachel nodded. More than anything, she wanted to throw herself in his arms, to feel the warmth and security of his embrace, but she didn't have the right.

"I'll be just down the hall if you need me." He pulled the door closed as he left.

She crumpled into a chair beside a fireplace filled with ferns for the summer, and fought back tears.

She felt alone.

Abandoned.

Frightened.

To calm herself, she closed her eyes and pictured her room at the ranch with its cozy furniture and friendly colors.

As soon as she closed her eyes, however, she was nodding off to sleep. She dragged herself to her feet, stripped off her clothes and tugged on her nightgown. With a prayer that things would look better in the morning, she crawled beneath the silk covers of the king-size bed and fell asleep.

SUNLIGHT SLANTING THROUGH an uncovered window awakened her the next morning. One bright beam fell on a sandstone sculpture of a Yorkshire terrier, curled on the marble hearth of the fireplace, so lifelike that for a moment she thought she saw it breathe.

She had always wanted a dog, but Ray wouldn't have one in the house.

She bolted upright in bed and gazed around the room. Her memories were returning. Not clear, crisp images with names and identification, but feelings and impressions. She recalled, for example, that she had detested this room with its satin draperies and ornate furnishings.

Throwing back the covers, she rose and went to the closet, a walk-in the size of her Montana bedroom. Row after row of designer dresses and expensive shoes lined the wall. She had disliked the clothes, too. Like her bedroom furnishings, all the choices had been Ray's.

Ray, her husband. Where was he?

Turning her back on the extravagant clothing, she hurried to the luggage she'd brought with her and pulled on a pair of jeans and a pale blue T-shirt. She slipped her feet into tennis shoes, tied the laces and headed for the door.

As she descended the wide staircase, she realized her memory of the house was returning. Downstairs at the end of the entry hall was a terrace where she and Ray had always had breakfast in good weather. Floating through the open French doors was the sound of voices, one male, one female.

Was it Ray? She wondered again why he hadn't been there to greet her last night. He'd *always* been there, critically overseeing her every move.

Her heart thumped with jittery anticipation, and she sighed with relief when she stepped onto the terrace. Wade, not Ray, sat at the wrought-iron table. In his faded jeans, chambray shirt and scuffed boots, he looked out of place on the formal terrace, but he appeared unintimidated by his posh surroundings. Marie had served his breakfast and was filling his coffee cup. As Rachel approached, he looked up with a warm smile that made her heart flip-flop with regret that she was married.

"Sleep well?" he asked.

"Yes, and I'm amazed to find I'm starving." She eyed the steaming blueberry pancakes he was devouring. "Any of those left?"

As if on cue, Marie returned, bearing a tray filled with pancakes, orange juice, coffee—and a large, bulky scrapbook.

"What's that?" Rachel indicated the thick volume.

Marie set the dishes before her and wiped her hands on her apron. "Mr. Lacy sent it over. Said you were to look at it. He figures it might stir your memories before he meets with you at ten this morning."

Intrigued, Rachel reached for the book, but Wade grasped her hand and shook his head. "Eat first. The memories can wait until later. Besides, I want to talk with you before I leave for the airport."

"Leave?" Rachel dropped her fork in alarm. "You're not really going?"

Wade looked around and shrugged. "I don't belong here..."

Rachel couldn't have agreed with him more. She didn't belong there, either. But unlike Wade, she had nowhere else to go.

"And I have a ranch to run," he added. "I can't impose much more on Leo."

Swallowing the lump in her throat at the thought of his departure, she dug into her breakfast. Her appetite, however, had disappeared. She sipped her juice and toyed with her pancakes before pushing her plate away.

"Please," she said, "I know it's asking a lot, but can't you stay at least another day?"

He sighed. "You know I'd like to, but under the circumstances…"

"My memories are coming back in bits and pieces." She suppressed a shudder. "It's very unsettling, and I could really use a friend right now."

Watching emotions scud across his face like storm clouds, she pleaded, "I have no right to ask you—"

"Ah, Rachel, you have every right. If you need me, I'll stay." His smile faded and he grimaced slightly. "I'd just rather not be around when *Mr.* Reid shows up. I think he's a heel for not being here last night to welcome you home, and if I run into him, I'll tell him so."

"Thank you. I owe you a great deal." She reached for the heavy volume Marie had laid beside her place. "I'd better get started if I'm to go through this before Mr. Lacy arrives."

She pulled the book toward her and flipped open the cover. Snapshots stared back at her from the first page.

Familiar faces that made her smile with elation.

"These are my parents," she cried. "I recognize them."

"The people from the dream you had on the mountain?" Wade asked gently.

Remembering the frightening dream, Rachel nodded, and turned the page with a shiver. She knew what was coming.

"Here's a picture of the house we lived in, and this one is of me and my dog, Scooty-poot." A Yorkshire terrier like the statue on the hearth upstairs. "I was only about five years old."

"Did you have brothers and sisters?" Wade asked.

She shook her head. "I was an only child."

She turned another page and was flooded with memories and nostalgia. In the photo, she stood with her parents on the steps of a mountain cabin. "This was the last vacation we ever took together, at Casey's Cove in the Smokey Mountains. Aunt Emily took me back there a time or two after my parents died, but it was never the same."

On the following page was a yellowed newspaper clipping with the headline, "Plane Crash in Chicago Kills 129."

"My parents died in that accident," she told him, feeling the pain of loss again as if for the first time. "I was only six. My great-aunt Emily took me in and raised me."

She turned the page. A studio portrait of a stiff, unsmiling woman glared up at her. "Yep, that's Aunt Emily. I don't think I ever saw her smile."

Memory after memory cascaded into her consciousness, one tumbling over the other until she had difficulty making sense of them. The scrapbook helped her place her recollections in chronological order. "See that big Victorian monstrosity?"

Wade glanced obliging at the photo.

"That was Aunt Emily's house. We lived there alone, just the two of us. The place terrified me."

"I can understand why," Wade said. "It looks haunted."

"I thought it was. It was full of creaks and squeaks and bumps in the night. I wanted to sleep with a night-light, but Aunt Emily wouldn't let me. Said it was a waste of electricity. She grew up during the Great Depression. It must have made her frugal."

"Is this you?" Wade pointed to a picture of a young woman in a prom dress. Admiration glinted in his eyes, and she remembered that he'd looked at her the same way the night of the barn dance, the night he'd held her in his arms....

Rachel blushed at the path her thoughts had taken. "That's me, right before the senior prom. Raymond Reid was my date."

"You were beautiful," Wade said, and she had to look away from the heat in his eyes. "You still are."

His compliment touched her, but it was taking them in a dangerous direction. Without responding, she turned another page. "Wedding pictures. Ray proposed after the prom. We were married a year later."

Wade's eyes held a hungry look as he gazed at her bridal photograph. "Raymond Reid is a damned lucky man."

Rachel flipped through a couple more pages. "That's funny. I can remember Ray's parents, the first house we lived in, the fact that Ray used to work for a courier company as a driver, but my memories stop there. This house is familiar, but I don't remember moving here."

Wade whistled. "For a delivery man, he made a hell of an income to afford a place like this."

Rachel frowned. "I don't remember anything about money, either."

Wade leaned closer, his eyes dark as if with pain. "Do you remember if you love him?"

"Ray? When I met him, I was just a kid, and I was crazy about him. Thought he was the handsomest man on earth and that I was the luckiest girl when he proposed. But now? It's puzzling. When I try to recall my feelings for Ray, there's nothing but this huge void."

Wade glanced at his watch. "It's almost ten o'clock. Maybe Mr. Lacy can fill in the blanks when he gets here."

She closed the album without looking at its final pages. "I'm anxious to hear what he has to say."

Carrying the scrapbook, she walked inside with Wade and down the long corridor toward the front of the house. The doorbell rang as they approached the entry, and Marie admitted Harold Lacy.

"We can talk in the study," Rachel said, after they'd exchanged greetings.

"I'll clear out while you two discuss business," Wade said.

"No!" Rachel grabbed his arm. "Please. I don't have anything to hide."

Besides, she figured it would be easier for Wade to hear the facts from Mr. Lacy than for her to repeat them to him later. She knew that what she felt for Wade wasn't one-sided. She'd seen the burning look in his eyes too many times to doubt that he cared for her. Wade deserved to hear the truth about her life as much as she did.

Wade's mouth twisted into a crooked grin. "Are you sure there's nothing to hide? Maybe there's something you haven't remembered."

"I can vouch for Jennifer," Lacy said in his cultured Southern voice. "There are no skeletons in her closet. If she has no objections to your sitting in on our conference, neither do I."

With a shrug, Wade acquiesced and followed Rachel and Lacy into a study at the front of the house, but she could tell from the tension in his shoulders he was as anxious as she was about what Lacy had to say.

Rachel surveyed the dark, heavy paneling and leather furniture with a shudder. She'd always felt uncomfortable in this room. Ray's room.

Lacy sat behind the massive desk, and Rachel and Wade settled in front of it in club chairs.

"First things first," the lawyer said. "When Sheriff Howard informed me, Jennifer, that your identity might have been assumed by a Ms. Rachel O'Riley, I was alarmed. I immediately had my clerks check your credit card and bank accounts. I am happy to report that Ms. O'Riley, however desperate she may be to elude her ex-fiancé, is obviously honest. There has been no activity in any of your accounts since the day before the train wreck."

"If she needs my money to escape him," Rachel said, "I hope she'll use it. I feel an affinity for someone trying to avoid a man she doesn't love."

"As well you would," Lacy stated cryptically.

"And Larry Crutchfield is lower than a snake," Wade said. "The woman's well rid of him."

"Despite your generous attitude, Jennifer," Lacy said with a smile, "Ms. O'Riley will be unable to access your accounts. I had them closed immediately."

"I wish her well," Rachel said. "My memories of her are starting to return—a pretty, vivacious woman with amazing strawberry-blond hair and a smattering of freckles. I thought her overtalkative at the time. In retrospect, I believe she was just nervous, with Crutchfield on her trail."

Lacy nodded toward the album she had laid on the desk. "Did you have time to peruse this?"

"I got as far as my wedding pictures and the first house Ray and I lived in. My memories up till then are clear. Afterwards is still pretty fuzzy."

"Then let's pick up where you left off," the attorney said, "and see if the rest of your memory can be restored."

He opened the album to the page where Rachel had ended her examination. "Shortly after you and Ray moved into your first house, your aunt Emily died suddenly of a stroke."

Rachel nodded sadly. "I remember. As strict as she had been with me, she loved me. She was my last living relative. Her death left me totally alone."

"What about your husband?" Wade asked softly, and Rachel smiled at him sadly. She knew what effort it had taken for him to ask the question, and how much he feared her answer. She wished she could show Mr. Lacy out, forget her past and lead Wade upstairs to the king-size bed—

"Raymond Reid." Lacy made a tsking sound and shook his head. "At the time Emily died, I made a terrible discovery. Raymond Reid had a cousin who had worked in my office. Long before Ray met you, Jennifer, this cousin divulged to him the details of your fortune."

"My fortune?" Rachel asked in surprise. "I don't remember that."

"When your parents died," the attorney explained, "they left huge life insurance policies, with you as the beneficiary. Your Aunt Emily and I were named as guardians and trustees in their will. Your aunt was an astute investor. By the time you were a senior in high school, your trust had grown into several million dollars."

Rachel felt as if she'd been socked in the stomach. "That much?"

"What did Rachel's—" Wade broke off, catching his mistake. "Er, Jennifer's fortune have to do with Ray?"

"Everything, unfortunately," Lacy said sadly. "The man wasn't interested in Jennifer. Only her money. Emily and I, however, were unaware at the time of his courtship that Ray knew of her fortune. No one else did except us."

A muscle ticked in Wade's jaw. "You're saying this Ray married Jennifer for her money?"

"Most definitely," Lacy said. "And his subsequent behavior proved it."

"What subsequent behavior?" Rachel asked breathlessly.

The attorney gazed at her with sad eyes. "Raymond Reid was a very controlling man. Apparently afraid that someone else might steal you, and especially your money, away, he kept you on a tight leash. Dictated everything about your life—where you would go, what you would wear, how you would furnish your house, who your friends would be—"

"And I let him?" Rachel asked in horror. She noted Wade's hands gripping the arms of his chair until his knuckles whitened. "What kind of a wimp was I?"

"Keep in mind, dear," Lacy said, "that when you married, you were only nineteen, all alone in the world and head over heels in love. Ray was older, bigger, stronger—and the only family you had. At first you gave in to his demands in an attempt to please him."

"At first?" Rachel asked. "And later?"

The attorney cleared his throat. "You wanted a divorce."

Wade leaned forward in his chair, and Rachel found breathing difficult. "Did I get it?"

"No."

"Why not?" The entire conversation had taken on a surrealistic cast. She remembered vaguely the things they were discussing, but she didn't *feel* them. It was almost as if they were talking about someone else.

"Ray refused," Lacy said. "He threatened to kill you if you left him."

"My God," Wade muttered under his breath, but loud enough for Rachel to hear.

"And Ray?" she asked, fearing the answer. "Where is he now?"

The attorney stared at her with searching eyes. "You really don't remember?"

Rachel shook her head.

Lacy took a deep breath. "Raymond Reid is dead."

Chapter Fourteen

Rachel sank back in her chair. Her initial reaction was relief. She was *free*. She could marry Wade, if he still wanted her. Then her confusion returned. "Ray is dead? Why can't I remember that?"

Lacy cocked an eyebrow. "You don't remember his death?"

She shook her head. "I only vaguely remember this house. Nothing after that."

"How did Mr. Reid die?" Wade asked quietly. Rachel could almost feel the dormant strength radiating from him, and was thankful again that he hadn't left her to handle these revelations alone. She wondered if he was as elated as she over her freedom, then realized with horror that she wasn't free at all until she learned the manner of Ray's death.

The attorney propped his fingertips together. "Let me back up a bit. It may help Jennifer remember."

"Please," Rachel agreed with a gesture that encompassed her surroundings. "Start with this monstrosity."

"Monstrosity?" Lacy asked.

"This ostentatious house." She caught Wade's

grin from the corner of her eye. Evidently he shared her assessment of the mansion. "Start from the time I moved here."

Lacy nodded. "That was several years ago. Ray had wanted a larger house from the day you were married. You finally convinced me to release enough money from your trust fund to purchase this place."

"I *wanted* this house?" she asked in disbelief.

The attorney smiled, and she felt a rush of affection for the old man. Uncle Harold. Her memories of him had returned in full, reminding her that he had been like a father to her since her parents' death.

"You hoped," Lacy said, "that if you gave Ray this house in the settlement, he would agree to divorce you."

"Apparently Ray wasn't buying that," Wade said dryly.

Rachel wondered if Wade was thinking what she was, wondered if he wanted her as badly this minute as she wanted him. She was free to love him, but she'd have to wait for his reaction until Uncle Harold had finished his story.

"You're absolutely right, Mr. Garrett. Raymond Reid was more avaricious and power hungry than any man I've ever met—and I've seen plenty of his ilk in my business. He didn't want part of your wealth, Jennifer. He wanted it all."

She shook her head slowly, trying to recall, but without any luck. "Why can't I remember this?"

"We'll call Dr. Sinclair," Wade suggested. "Maybe she can explain what's going on with your memories."

Rachel shot him a look of gratitude, but had to turn away from the heat in his eyes before she forgot herself and embarrassed Uncle Harold.

"Excellent suggestion, Mr. Garrett," the lawyer said. "Now to return to our saga. As the stock market boomed in the nineties, your fortune, Jennifer, grew geometrically. The more money you acquired, the less inclined Ray was to grant your divorce."

"I don't understand," Rachel said. "Why didn't I just walk out on him?"

Lacy gazed at her with sympathy in his eyes. "You truly don't remember, do you? Raymond Reid was a horrible man with a violent temper. You feared for your life."

"Why didn't she—or you, for that matter—report him to the police?" Wade asked.

"Ray was not only greedy and power hungry, he was extremely intelligent," the lawyer said. "His threats against Jennifer were never direct, always insinuations. Nothing overt enough to justify a restraining order. I guess you could say he practiced psychological terrorism."

Rachel winced at the anger suffusing Wade's face. She'd never seen him so enraged, not even the time Jordan had burned his timber.

"So you just let Rach—Jennifer suffer?" Wade looked like he wanted to smash something.

"On the contrary," Lacy said, obviously unperturbed by Wade's controlled fury. "Jennifer and I had a plan, one in which she would file for divorce and disappear to a place where Ray would never find her."

"So I *did* divorce him," Rachel said with a sigh of relief.

"No," Lacy said. "Ray died before we could activate our plan."

Emotionally exhausted, Rachel slumped in her chair. No matter how hard she tried, she couldn't remember the events or circumstances her attorney described.

"How did Ray die?" Wade asked again.

A terrifying possibility presented itself, and Rachel sat bolt upright. "Oh, my God, *I* didn't...?"

"No, you didn't harm him." Lacy rose from the desk, circled to the front and perched on the edge.

Wade reached across the space between their chairs and grasped her hand. She appreciated the reassuring warmth of his grip, the one element that seemed real in a world gone topsy-turvy. She never wanted to let him go.

"You and Ray were on vacation in the Cayman Islands last December," the attorney continued. "Ray insisted on scuba diving, even though he'd had too much to drink. You never liked boats, so you returned to the hotel. Divers found Ray's body the next day."

"That was December," she said. "What did I do for the last six months, before the train wreck?"

"There were hundreds of details to attend to," the lawyer said. "Funeral arrangements, executing Ray's will, putting this house on the market..."

Rachel smiled for the first time since Harold Lacy had begun his story. "I knew I wouldn't keep this place."

"Where was Rachel going when her train crashed?" Wade asked.

"Seattle," Lacy explained. "She wanted to start a new life with a clean slate. Find her own identity after so many years under Ray's thumb."

The whole story sounded to Rachel like someone else's life. She couldn't understand why she could remember up to a certain point and no further. She felt the encouraging pressure of Wade's grip, and her heart soared with happiness. She was free to love him now. Free to marry.

But not into a "strictly business" arrangement. She'd already made one bad marriage. She wouldn't repeat her mistake. She wouldn't marry another man who didn't love her. If she was to marry Wade, she had to be one hundred percent certain of his love. She thought Wade loved her, but she had to be sure.

"Maybe we should call Dr. Sinclair now," Wade suggested.

"Just a few more details first, please." The attorney opened his briefcase and removed a few items. "I obtained a new copy of your driver's license and other identification, and here are your new credit cards and checkbook. If you have any questions, give me a call."

Instinctively, Rachel stood and hugged the old man, who was the closest thing she had to a relative. "Thank you, Uncle Harold."

"Ah," he said with a satisfied smile, returning her embrace, "that you do remember." He turned to Wade. "I appreciate all you've done for Jennifer, and especially extending your visit while she gets her bearings again."

Wade's gaze met hers. His eyes were filled with unspoken promises. ''I'll do whatever I can to make her happy.''

Rachel and Wade showed the attorney out, and when she closed the door behind him, she silently echoed his appreciation of Wade Garrett.

She didn't want to think about what life would be like when Wade returned to Montana and she was left in the gargantuan house all alone.

WADE FOUND RACHEL on the terrace later that afternoon, flipping through the pages of the album Mr. Lacy had put together to stir her memories.

''Remember anything more?'' he asked.

She shook her head. ''But at least since talking with Dr. Sinclair, I understand why not.''

''You finally got hold of her?''

Rachel nodded. ''She thinks the block on that portion of my memories comes from the emotional trauma I suffered, first from Ray's abuse, then from the horror of the train wreck.''

Wade still hadn't come down from the elated high he'd experienced when he'd learned that she was free. Free to love him. Free to marry him. He wanted to gather her in his arms and hold her forever. She deserved better, especially after the terrible years she'd spent with Raymond Reid. But he realized, too, how emotionally vulnerable she was right now, still struggling to retrieve the remainder of her history before the train wreck. He didn't want to spook her by making love to her if she wasn't ready. ''Did the doctor say whether you will ever get those memories back?''

"Dr. Sinclair says I'm guarding my emotions because subconsciously I'm afraid of being hurt again. If I ever feel safe enough to allow myself to feel things deeply once more, the memories will probably return."

Her hair glinted with highlights of gold in the afternoon sun, and Wade remembered when he'd first seen her, with her golden hair the color of his palomino and eyes the hue of spring leaves. He'd learned much more about her since. She had an inexhaustible capacity for love, as she'd demonstrated with Jordan. She had courage and tenacity, and refused to allow any adversity to keep her down. She might not remember her life with Ray Reid—and from the oppressiveness of it, that was probably just as well—but somewhere along the line, she had learned some hard lessons and revitalized her self-esteem.

"In the meantime," Wade suggested, "I suggest we give Marie the night off and get out of this mausoleum."

"You won't get any protests from me."

"I've been doing some investigating this afternoon. Not too far from here, down by the river, there's a fish camp famous for their fried catfish, hush puppies, juke box and dance floor. Want to give it a try?"

Her glorious smile rewarded him for all the calls he'd made to discover the fish place. "Absolutely. But only if you'll let me buy."

"You may be a millionaire, Ms. Reid, but I have a grub stake of my own. This is my treat."

Her sunny laughter rang across the marble stones of the terrace. "It's a deal."

He felt like whooping with joy. Only this morning, he had been anxious to leave Memphis. He hadn't wanted to meet the mysterious Raymond Reid, and he damned well hadn't wanted to prolong the agony of parting from Rachel.

Things had happened too fast the past few days for him to have much time to think. First the sleeper fire, then Crutchfield's return and the discovery of Rachel's identity.

Wade hadn't had time to dwell on the fact that when he'd shared Maggie's story with Rachel, her acceptance and understanding had melted the glacier that had encased his heart since his wife's death. Now he was free to love again. And he did. He loved Rachel, aka Jennifer Reid, with all his heart and soul. The only problem would be convincing her, after his cockeyed proposal of marriage, that his love was genuine and not some crazy business scheme.

He grinned with a smile that filled him right down to his boots. He'd always loved a challenge. He fully intended to take Rachel with him when he returned to Montana.

Grabbing her hand, he tugged her toward the front of the house, where he'd parked the rental car. "We don't have to wait for suppertime. I don't get back East often, so I'd like to do some sightseeing. You game?"

"Are you kidding? I'm up for anything that will get me out of this house."

HOURS LATER, after Wade had driven the rental car back up the driveway of the Reid mansion, Rachel stepped out of the car and stood staring at the star-studded sky. A cool breeze, laden with the scent of magnolia blossoms, blew in from the Mississippi. Only the rustle of leaves and the plaintive call of a whippoorwill broke the midnight silence. Only one more thing was needed, Rachel thought, to make the night perfect. She wanted to make love with Wade, to sleep with him, to wake up the next morning to see his face on the pillow beside her.

"This has been the happiest day of my life," she said. "I can't remember ever having so much fun."

Wade joined her and draped his arm around her shoulders. "I can't remember ever eating so much or dancing so long. I had a great time."

She had never laughed so long or felt so completely at ease with a man. It was as if she'd known Wade Garrett all her life. "I don't want it to end."

He turned her to face him, dark passion glowing in his eyes. "It doesn't have to."

"But you're going back to Montana tomorrow—"

"Come with me."

Her heart jumped with longing. To return to the land she'd come to treasure, to the child she'd learned to cherish, with the man she'd fallen desperately in love with was too much to hope for.

"I couldn't."

Her quick objection surprised her until she realized she feared committing herself to marriage before her other memories returned. She also had to be certain Wade loved her as much as she hoped he did. As much as she wanted to return to the ranch with him, she knew she needed time. Time to make sure she didn't make another mistake.

"Mr. Lacy can take care of things for you here—"

"It isn't that."

His mahogany-colored eyes glowed with heat, even in the darkness. "If you're worried that I still want you as some kind of business partner..."

She pulled away from him, afraid of being swayed by his nearness. "We should go inside to discuss this."

Heading toward the front door, she suddenly remembered the one place on the property she had felt was her own space. "Follow me."

Skirting the building, she opened an iron gate to a flagstone pathway that edged the side of the house. At the rear of the mansion, the path continued deep into the formal garden. The walkway was dimly lit, but her memory now was strong. She could have navigated her way in total darkness.

She stopped in front of a screen-enclosed gazebo, hidden from the house by a grove of trees. "We can talk in here. This was my private spot. Ray never came here."

Wade followed her up the steps into the octagonal room. She switched on a table lamp and gazed around in satisfaction. Someone—Marie?—had kept the gazebo spotlessly clean and just as she had left it. Deep wicker chairs filled with overstuffed cushions were grouped before a fireplace. The room was filled with potted ferns, palms and weeping fig trees, like a desert oasis.

She scrabbled in the drawer of a table, found matches and lighted scented candles on the low table before the sofa and on the mantel. With the flick of a switch, soft music issued from a hidden sound system.

Wade pulled her into his arms. "May I have this dance—for the rest of my life?"

"Won't your feet get tired?" she teased.

"Not as long as you're in my arms."

She clung to him, inhaling his male, earthy scent, while every objection to returning to Montana with him flew from her mind. As they danced, he pulled her closer, until her body molded to his. She could feel his heat, how much he wanted her, even through layers of clothing.

"God, I love you, Rachel." His breath warmed her ear. "Say you'll marry me."

Leaning back in his arms, she glimpsed the passion glowing in his eyes. Before she could respond to his proposal, his mouth covered hers, and the cool night air seemed to explode around them, as if ignited by fire. He devoured her with kisses, explored her mouth with his tongue, nipped her neck with his teeth.

They sank to the Oriental carpet that covered the gazebo floor. He lifted his hands to the buttons on her shirt, then paused. "Let me make love to you."

She didn't hesitate. "Please."

With a haste that was almost humorous, they pushed their clothes aside. She shuddered with desire when he caressed her with his large, strong hands, electrifying every nerve he grazed. His lips followed where his hands had touched. She didn't have all her memories, but she knew without doubt no one had ever moved her as Wade Garrett did now.

Her earlier reservations vanished like mist beneath the sun. She wanted him with an intensity that surprised and pleased her. One look into his striking eyes, and she knew they belonged together. His eager expression, his hungry mouth, his persuasive hands told her he cherished her.

Passion numbed her consciousness until she could only think how much she wanted him. He drew her against his body, and the contact of their naked flesh caused years of repressed desire to burst free.

This man who had cared for her through the trauma of amnesia while allowing her to keep her self-respect, meant the world to her. As she ran her fingers through his hair and gazed into his eyes, she wanted to give him as much as he'd given her. She drew a teasing finger down his cheek to the pulse throbbing in his neck, and tugged him closer. He dipped his head, nuzzled her ear, and she quivered with longing.

"Now," she begged.

"Ah, Rachel," he whispered against her lips, "I could never refuse you anything."

With swift tenderness, he pressed her to the carpet and lowered himself atop her. She gasped with delight when he entered her. Her heart leaped, faltered, then matched the pulsing rhythm of his body as he moved with her.

Her ecstasy heightened as she glimpsed the stark and sensuous passion on his face. Bonded with him, their bodies glistening with perspiration, she felt as if they were flying, rising higher and higher, until the stars shone below them and the magnolia-scented air seemed too rare to breathe. His cry at climax melded with hers, a crescendo of consummate pleasure.

Sated, he settled beside her and drew her into the crook of his arm. She snuggled against him as if she'd always belonged there.

"I love you, Rachel. I always will."

She gazed into his dark eyes with complete happiness. "I love you, too."

"Maybe now you'll answer my question."

She pretended confusion. "What question is that?"

Without warning, a myriad memories suddenly opened up, lurching one atop the other, sucking her into a vortex of unhappy and terrifying recollections. She cried out, as if in pain.

Alarmed, Wade sat up and pulled her to him. "What's wrong?"

She struggled to breathe, suffocated by the weight of memories she'd rather forget. Every miserable second she'd spent as Ray's wife whirled through her brain, battering her with the pain and unhappiness she'd suffered through the years. She'd never been allowed to make a decision, express an opinion, to choose her own friends. Her entire life had been regimented to Ray's plan, an agenda that she was forced to follow to the letter or suffer horrible verbal and emotional abuse. She had been Ray's wife. Her own identity had been erased in the process. She didn't know who she really was.

For the first time in her life, she had opened herself fully to someone, unleashed her emotions and, as a result, freed her repressed memories.

"I remember," she said, when she was finally able to draw breath. "Everything."

She couldn't stop trembling. Wade draped an afghan from the sofa around her and held her close, rocking her in his arms, smoothing her hair and whispering gentle encouragement in her ear.

Slowly her breathing returned to normal and her shivering eased. She rose from his arms and tugged on her clothes, unable to meet his gaze.

He dressed quickly. Turning her toward him, he lifted her chin until she had to meet his eyes. A frown wrinkled his forehead and his expression was concerned. "You're not sorry we..."

She nodded sadly. "But only because I'll know what I'm missing."

Alarm and bewilderment replaced the concern in his gaze. "What are you saying?"

She took a deep breath and released it, buying time while she gathered her courage. "I can't marry you, Wade."

"But you said you loved me."

She traced her fingers along the line of his jaw. "I do. I always will."

"Then why..."

She sighed again and pulled away. Sinking into a chair, she clasped her hands in front of her. "Being married to Raymond Reid was a nightmare. I never developed my own identity, never learned what *I* wanted from life. Please try to understand. Even though all my memories have returned, I don't know who I am. It wouldn't be fair for me to marry you under those circumstances.''

He knelt in front of her. ''I'm willing to take that chance.''

She smiled and ruffled his hair. ''I'm not. Maggie hurt you terribly. I don't want to be the one to hurt you again.''

He stood and pulled her into his arms. She fought with every bit of self-control to keep from yielding to his embrace.

''I need you, Rachel. Jordan needs you.''

She shook her head sadly and pulled away. ''I was on my way to start a new life in Seattle, to forge my own identity, when the train derailed. I still have to find myself before I make any lifetime commitments.''

''Then you're not saying you'll never marry me?'' His expression was hopeful.

She felt as if her heart was shattering, but knew she was doing the right thing. ''Don't wait for me, Wade. You need someone to love you, and Jordan needs a mother.''

A mixture of pain and anger flashed across his face before he turned on his heel and left the gazebo.

She sank back into her chair and sobbed. She knew she was right, but why did being right have to hurt so badly?

Chapter Fifteen

Three months later

Rachel stared out the window at the gloomy, rainy Seattle day. Luckily, Kitty's Corner Bookshop, where she worked, was always cheerful with its shelves of colorful books, its cozy nooks and corners filled with overstuffed chairs, flowers and plants, with plenty of good light for reading. Potpourri scented the air and blended pleasantly with the tang of newly printed pages.

The bell over the front door jingled, and Kitty Conover, the store's owner, entered. She furled her dripping umbrella, placed it by the door and shucked her sopping raincoat.

"Mail's here, Rachel," she called. "Take a break. You have a letter."

Rachel deserted the shelves she was restocking. "It must be from Uncle Harold."

Kitty, a plump woman in her fifties with graying hair and smiling eyes, shook her head. "This one's postmarked Montana."

After pouring a cup of Russian tea from the ever-

present pot warmed by a quilted cozy, she handed
it to Rachel, along with the letter, slightly damp
from the rain.

"Take your time," Kitty said. "Enjoy your letter."

Rachel curled in a window seat at the back of the
shop, placed her cup and saucer beside her and con-
templated the envelope, addressed in Jordan's child-
ish scrawl. The letter, she knew from experience,
would be printed from his computer.

Jordan had written her faithfully once a week
since the day she and Wade had parted in Memphis.
She had made Wade promise not to contact her, but
he'd managed to convince her to correspond with
Jordan, explaining that the young boy wouldn't understand her abandonment.

Hell, Wade had said, he didn't understand it himself, but he was willing to abide by Rachel's wishes
as long as she didn't break Jordan's heart, too.

Rachel always found Jordan's letters bittersweet.
She loved hearing what the boy was doing, and especially his accounts of his father's activities, but
they left her feeling homesick and discontent for
hours—until she managed to throw herself into the
activities of her new life. And until the next letter
arrived.

Dear Rachel,
We had some snow last week, but the sun came
out and melted it away pretty quick. I was glad,
'cause I'm working on my rock collection. Dad
is helping me. I will enter it in the competition
next month at the County Harvest Festival.

Last weekend, Dad sold a bunch of his cows at auction. They brought a good price, but it didn't make Dad happy like it used to. Dad never seems happy since you left us. When are you coming back? Dad says I'm not supposed to ask you, but I was hoping you could be here for the festival to see my rock exhibit.

I hope I spelled everything right. I used the spell checker on my computer.

Love,
Jordan

Rachel smoothed away a tear with her index finger and glanced up to find Kitty staring at her over her own steaming mug of tea.

"Why do you read those letters?" Kitty asked. "They always make you cry."

Rachel had told Kitty her whole story shortly after Kitty hired her, because the woman had become her friend as well as her employer.

"He's just a little boy. He won't understand if I don't answer him."

"Well, I'm an old lady, and I don't understand, either," Kitty said with a grimace, settling onto the window seat beside Rachel. "If I were you, I'd be making tracks for Montana the fastest way I could get there."

"But I—"

Kitty held up her hand. "I know. After being married to Ray, you're afraid of being a doormat all your life."

"That's why I came here," Rachel said defensively. "To take charge of my life."

"Honey, did Wade Garrett hold a gun to your head when he proposed?"

"Of course not."

"Did he ever beat you?"

"No!"

"Verbally abuse you?"

Rachel shook her head.

"Tell you how to run your life?"

"And your point is?"

"That if you married him, it would be of your own free will, wouldn't it?"

"Yes, but…"

Kitty regarded her with kind eyes. "The best way to avoid being a doormat *is* to take charge of your life. Do what *you* want to do. If you're not marrying a man you love because of Raymond Reid, then he's still controlling you from the grave."

Rachel flinched at Kitty's piercing words. "I never thought of it that way before."

"Well, maybe it's time you did." The bell jingled over the shop door, and Kitty stood. "Finish your tea, then back to work. We've got customers."

WADE TURNED THE COLLAR of his denim jacket up to ward off the stiff north breeze, and headed from the barn toward the house. He pulled up short when he found Jordan huddled on the front steps, shivering in the cold, his face streaked with tears.

He lowered himself beside the boy. "What's wrong, son?"

Jordan shook his head and swiped at his face with the sleeve of his jacket. "I know boys aren't supposed to cry. I'm sorry, Dad."

Wade put his arm around his son and tugged him close. "How about sharing your problem with your old man?"

"It's Rachel." Jordan tried to swallow a sob, but didn't succeed.

Fear struck Wade and ricocheted down his spine. Jordan had been his only line of communication with Rachel since the fateful day he'd left her in Memphis. "Is she ill?"

Jordan shook his head. "No, Rachel's fine. She loves that bookstore where she works. She even sent me the whole set of Harry Potter books."

Wade breathed a sigh of relief. "Then what's the trouble?"

"Tomorrow's the festival, and Rachel won't be here to see my rock collection." Jordan lifted his tear-stained face, and his obvious unhappiness wrenched Wade's heart. The boy began sobbing openly and buried his face in Wade's jacket. "I'm sorry, Dad. I know you don't want me to be a sissy crybaby, but I can't help it. I miss Rachel so much."

Wade clasped his son tightly against his chest. "Go ahead and cry, Jordan. I've shed quite a few tears over Rachel myself."

His confession shocked Jordan's tears away. "Gosh, *you* cried? But I thought grown men aren't supposed to cry."

Tears welled in Wade's eyes. "Some things, like Rachel, are worth crying over, son. I love her and miss her, just like you do."

The screen door slammed behind them as Ursula stepped out of the house onto the porch, tugging her sweater tightly around her. "Don't you two have more sense than to sit out here in the cold? I've made hot chocolate and—''

She broke off at the sound of a car coming up the drive from the main road. ''You expecting company?''

Wade stood and pulled Jordan up beside him. ''Go on in, son. It's probably those damned Realtors. I'll get rid of them.''

He had started down the steps toward the approaching car when he heard Jordan shout behind him and thunder down the stairs. ''It's Rachel!''

Wade's heart somersaulted in his chest before he stomped down hard on his rising anticipation. Afraid some blond real estate agent had falsely raised Jordan's hopes, Wade grabbed his son by the collar as the boy headed for the slowing car. ''Hold up, Jordan. It isn't—''

The car stopped and the door opened. Rachel, dressed in jeans and a pullover sweater the color of her eyes, and looking even more beautiful than Wade had remembered, stepped out.

With a joyful shout, Wade released Jordan. They both raced toward her, and Rachel ran to meet them. Wade scooped her into his arms. Their lips met, and the taste of her sent his blood roaring through his veins. Jordan wrapped his arms around both their legs, hugging for all he was worth.

Coming up for air, Wade pulled back and gazed into Rachel's laughing eyes.

''Still looking for a mother for this kid?'' she asked playfully.

''Sure am. But only under one condition.''

Her expression sobered. "Not a strictly business proposition?"

"No way," Wade said. "Only under the condition that you let me love you for the rest of my life."

Rachel laughed aloud. "Sounds like a heck of a deal to me."

Their lips met again, and Wade was only dimly aware of Jordan running in circles around them and whooping with joy, and of Ursula beaming happily from the porch.

"What made you change your mind?" Wade asked.

Rachel smiled. "I realized when I found myself that I was lost without you and Jordan."

"We're a real family now," Jordan cried happily. "Aren't we, Dad?"

"There's one thing missing," Rachel said.

"What?" Wade asked in alarm.

"I've always wanted a dog."

"Rachel, darlin', if it makes you happy, we'll open a kennel."

With one arm around Rachel, the other around his son, and his heart overflowing, Wade led them toward the house.

* * * * *

Don't miss Charlotte Douglas's follow up
to
MONTANA MAIL-ORDER WIFE,

STRANGER IN HIS ARMS,

coming next month from
Harlequin Intrigue.

For a sneak preview, read the teaser
on the next page...

Chapter One

Slinging her hastily filled backpack over her shoulder, she raced toward the front door, but skidded to a stop before she reached it. A huge figure on the porch was silhouetted against the etched glass of the door.

He had come for her.

Pivoting on her heel, she sprinted to the back of the house, eased out the door noiselessly and ran across the backyard. Just as she was clambering up the fence to gain access to the alley, the neighbor's dog howled.

Running footsteps thundered behind her and a hand grasped her ankle as she hoisted herself over the fencetop. With a fierce kick that contacted with flesh and bone and elicited a curse from her pursuer, she freed herself and dropped into the alleyway.

Without a backward look, she kicked up dust as she sped toward the main street, clogged with going-to-work traffic. Just as she reached the curb, a bus approached.

There is a God, she thought, and breathed a prayer of thanks.

The bus slowed and stopped, and she hopped on. The doors closed behind her, and the bus gained speed.

Only then did she dare risk a look behind.

He stood on the curb for an instant, glowering with rage, then sprinted toward his car, parked in front of her house. Her only hope was to exit the bus without him catching her.

And if she could pull that off, she needed to disappear.

Permanently.

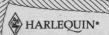

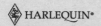

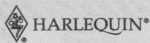

If you enjoyed what you just read,
then we've got an offer you can't resist!

Take 2 bestselling love stories FREE!

Plus get a FREE surprise gift!

Harlequin invites you to walk down the aisle...

To honor our year long celebration of weddings, we are offering an exciting opportunity for you to own the Harlequin Bride Doll. Handcrafted in fine bisque porcelain, the wedding doll is dressed for her wedding day in a cream satin gown accented by lace trim. She carries an exquisite traditional bridal bouquet and wears a cathedral-length dotted Swiss veil. Embroidered flowers cascade down her lace overskirt to the scalloped hemline; underneath all is a multi-layered crinoline.

Join us in our celebration of weddings by sending away for your own Harlequin Bride Doll. This doll regularly retails for $74.95 U.S./approx. $108.68 CDN. One doll per household. Requests must be received no later than June 30, 2001. Offer good while quantities of gifts last. Please allow 6-8 weeks for delivery. Offer good in the U.S. and Canada only. Become part of this exciting offer!

Simply complete the order form and mail to:
"A Walk Down the Aisle"

IN U.S.A
P.O. Box 9057
3010 Walden Ave.
Buffalo, NY 14240-9057

IN CANADA
P.O. Box 622
Fort Erie, Ontario
L2A 5X3

Enclosed are eight (8) proofs of purchase found on the last page of every specially marked Harlequin series book and $3.75 check or money order (for postage and handling). Please send my Harlequin Bride Doll to:

Name (PLEASE PRINT)

Address   Apt. #

City   State/Prov.   Zip/Postal Code

Account # (if applicable)   **098 KIK DAEW**

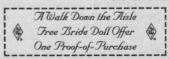

A Walk Down the Aisle
Free Bride Doll Offer
One Proof-of-Purchase

Visit us at www.eHarlequin.com

PHWDAPOP